You're the One
that I Want

You're the One
that I Want

Angela Britnell

A Delicious Selection of Bite Size Reads!

Copyright © 2016 Angela Britnell

Published 2016 by Choc Lit Limited
Penrose House, Crawley Drive, Camberley, Surrey GU15 2AB, UK
www.choc-lit.com

The right of Angela Britnell to be identified as the Author of this
Work has been asserted by her in accordance with the Copyright,
Designs and Patents Act 1988

A CIP catalogue record for this book is available
from the British Library

ISBN: 978-1-78189-354-8

Printed and bound by Clays Ltd

This story simply had to be dedicated to my indomitable mother-in-law, Jo, former tour guide and worldwide traveller, with happy memories of the first ever coach trip I took with her. I still look out for a red umbrella waving guide whenever I see a tour group!

Acknowledgements

Thank you to the Tasting Panel readers who passed
You're the One that I Want and made this possible:
Celia M., Hrund, Claire W., Karen M., Lizzie D.,
Linda W., Heather S., Alma and Isabelle.

Chapter One

'A coach trip around Europe? Seriously?' Matt couldn't hide his dismay. He'd been thinking along the lines of an expensive piece of jewellery or a new flat screen television.

'You told me I could choose whatever I wanted for my retirement present.' His mother's glare was the same one she'd kept legions of pupils in line with for the last forty years. 'I want to spend time with you.' The words "uninterrupted by your work" went unsaid.

Matt didn't care for the word workaholic but building an extremely successful business didn't lend itself to regular eight-hour days. He'd have to pick his words with care to get out of this without upsetting his mother. 'It sure isn't a great time for me to take off. You know we're opening another branch of TekSpeak in Atlanta in June.'

'When will it be convenient?' Cecily snapped. '2025? 2035? I'd prefer to go while I can still walk unaided and have all my faculties if you don't mind.'

He needed to change his plan of attack. 'Why a coach trip? I've got a friend who owns a fancy spa resort in the Napa Valley. We could fly out there for a long weekend of being pampered.'

'If I'd wanted that I'd have asked for it in the first place. And no I don't want a luxury cruise or a month in Australia.'

Thank the Lord.

'I've always wanted to get to Europe and a coach

trip will be perfect. Everything is organised and we'll meet lots of interesting people.'

To a natural introvert like Matt the thought of being shuffled around with a group of talkative strangers from place to place with no means of escape was his idea of hell on earth, but he held his tongue.

'I've picked the one I want to go on. Page eight.' She thrust a brochure at him. 'Lots of their last minute trips are on sale and this one's a real bargain so the extra optional excursions shouldn't break your bank.' The touch of sarcasm hung in the air between them. They both knew money wasn't the issue.

Matt's heart sunk even further as he scanned over the trip details. The title said it all. European Speed Date. Seven countries in ten days. It reminded him of the old comedy film, *If It's Tuesday, This Must Be Belgium*, and not in a good way.

'Please, dear.' The wobble in her voice got to him and Matt found himself agreeing. A small flash of triumph brightened his mother's face and Matt knew he'd been well and truly had.

Sarah could barely control her excitement. 'Are you serious? We won?' The moment she stepped in the door her mother had rushed out of the kitchen waving an envelope and grinning from ear to ear.

'Any holiday we want from their last minute deals section! I don't know how we're going to choose!' Betty exclaimed.

They loved competitions. It didn't matter if it was crosswords, making up advertising slogans or the chance to win a year's supply of dog food (despite not owning a dog) and their new faster internet connection had opened up even more opportunities. A lot of Sarah's friends couldn't understand why she'd moved back in with her mother but a year ago it'd made sense. They'd always got on well and when Sarah's father died unexpectedly about the same time as her blink-and-you'd-miss-it marriage failed it'd seemed an obvious choice to make. Along with stretching her salary from running the local nursery school it'd been a comfort for them both.

'I've boiled the kettle and I treated us to a cream cake each from the bakery. Take your coat off and sit down so we can look at the brochure together.' A guilty expression crossed her mother's face. 'I did sneak a quick look when it arrived but I won't say a word. Promise.'

Sarah ignored the chocolate éclair and allowed her tea to go cold while she flipped through pages of glossy pictures and tempting descriptions of all the trips on offer. If she hadn't inherited her mother's fair skin she'd have plumped for going to Spain and Portugal, imagining herself returning with a flattering golden tan instead of the reality of bright pink sunburn. As she turned the page Sarah couldn't help smiling.

'It has to be this one doesn't it?' She pointed. 'I know it'll be rather a rush but the dates fit in perfectly with my Easter holidays. Seven countries, including England, and all those different cities. It'll be amazing and how can we not take the chance to spend a day in Venice?' Her mother's skin paled. 'Would you rather go on one that concentrates on one place?'

'Don't be silly.' She reached over and patted Sarah's hand. 'Of course I chose the same one.'

Both women fell quiet and no words were needed

to spell out what was foremost in both their minds. They'd give anything for Sarah's father to be planning the holiday with them because he'd been born in a small village near Venice.

'That's decided then,' Betty declared in a no-nonsense tone.

'I could really do with getting away.' Ten days away from the ever-present black cloud of bumping into her ex-husband around the village would be amazing. Tim's father owned the local garage and Tim with his friendly, confident manner was a car salesman to his fingertips. His involvement in everything from the pub darts team to playing the lead role in the local pantomime made him hard to avoid around St. Trewin. 'The weather might be unpredictable but I'll take a chance if you will?'

Her mother's quick, warm hug said it all.

'Fresh tea,' Sarah said and jumped up from the sofa.

While the kettle boiled she leaned against the countertop and allowed her smile to fade. This holiday would give her a breathing space before fulfilling her mental promise to re-evaluate her life after a year at home. Sarah filled the teapot and selected a couple of clean mugs.

'Tea's up.' Brandishing their hot drinks she left the kitchen and determined not to spoil her mother's good mood.

Chapter Two

Rainy, cold days were the bane of anyone with a noisy, active toddler but Sarah had thirty to contend with, making today's ten-hour stint at the nursery school endless. They'd had a week of appalling weather and everyone was fed up because there were only so many puzzles, crafts and books they could do to fill the time. A dull headache pulled at her temples as she locked up but Sarah glanced at the calendar and smiled. Only another eight days before she'd be escaping from cold, wet Cornwall. Probably to equally cold, wet continental Europe but Sarah's optimistic side asserted itself and she determined to be positive.

Having lived in St. Trewin all her life the walk from one end of the village meant frequent stops to speak to people she knew so it took ages. As she passed the church a speeding car hit a puddle and splashed up to soak her legs. She stepped inside the warm house with relief and smelled the fragrant aromas of her favourite beef stew cooking.

'Mum, I'm home,' she called out, 'I'm going to change.' Sarah hung up her wet mac and kicked off her soggy shoes before running upstairs to her bedroom. Stripping off she pulled on a nice thick jumper, clean jeans and her cosy sheepskin slippers and hurried down to the kitchen.

'Hello, love.' Betty glanced around from the stove. 'We got the confirmation for our holiday. Do you fancy going into town on Saturday? I could do with a few new things to wear in the evenings. I don't want to let you down.'

Sarah hugged her mum. 'You could never do that and it's not like we're going on a fancy cruise. I don't think people will dress up much.' She hoped she was right. All her savings were going into the account mentally labelled "Sarah's Escape" and she didn't intend on breaking into it for the sake of clothes she didn't need. She was going purely to see the sights and enjoy her mother's company, not to impress anyone with her fashion sense or lack of it.

'Oh. Pity.'

Sarah quickly backtracked. She couldn't be mean. 'We can go shopping if you like. I could probably do with a couple of new tops.'

'Good. I'll treat you for an early birthday present.' Betty's smile returned. 'Let's have our tea.' She carried on dishing up and plumped a couple of fluffy dumplings on top of each steaming bowl of stew.

Sarah sensed her mother watching her as she started to eat and put down her spoon. 'What's up?'

Betty frowned. 'I didn't know whether to say anything or not, love, but I think I should. When I went into the hairdresser's this morning Mavis and Vera were talking under the dryers but they stopped when they saw me. Then Deirdre Bunt came in and you know she's not one to mince words.' *Not like you, Mum.* 'She asked if I'd heard about Tim.'

Sarah's heart thumped. 'What about Tim?' Her mother pushed her stew around the bowl.

'Althea's pregnant.'

Hot tears pressed at her eyes. As if the humiliation

6

of her husband running off with her so-called best friend wasn't bad enough.

'Deirdre said Tim was bragging to anyone who would listen in the Queen's Head last night.'

Bile rose in Sarah's throat. He'd never wanted children, or at least not with her. Tim said he preferred it to be the two of them on their own for a while and that they had plenty of time to think about starting a family. She'd gone along with him to keep the peace.

'When's the baby due?' Her steady voice impressed even herself.

'Er, I think around September. '

I hope it'll be a boiling hot summer and she's waddling around like a beached whale. She considered her unkind thoughts a generous reaction in the circumstances. 'I'm glad you told me. I'd rather be prepared.' *Prepared?*

'There's something else.' Two bright red spots of heat coloured her mother's cheeks. 'They're getting married on Easter Saturday.'

Sarah's throat tightened and she forced out a reply. 'In our church?' *Please say no. Please tell me he's not going to marry her in the same place where he pledged his undying love to me less than three years ago.* Her mother's nod was all it took for her control to crack. A single tear escaped and trickled down her face before she roughly brushed it away. 'Thank goodness we won't be here.' She picked up her spoon and scooped up a large bite of stew. 'This is delicious.' Sarah forced herself to swallow.

Later, in the privacy of her own bedroom her poor pillow would be the recipient of another late-night sobbing session but for now she'd pretend indifference.

No way did she want Tim back but the failure of her short marriage still hurt. The expression "charming the birds from the trees" was surely invented for men like her ex-husband. As a teenager Sarah was the only girl for miles around who didn't fall for his dazzling smile and blond good looks. When she returned to work in the village school he'd relentlessly pursued her until she finally agreed to a date. He'd wooed her with everything in his romantic arsenal until she believed herself to be in love and accepted his proposal. Almost as soon as they were married he lost interest and fell back into his old habits; flirting came as easy to him as breathing and he saw nothing wrong in it. He'd accused her of being no fun and tried to make out it was her own fault when he got tempted by her bubbly best friend.

'What are you looking forward to most, Mum? Apart from Venice I can't wait to see Paris. I know it probably won't be as wonderful as I imagine but I don't care.'

Sarah knew her mother wasn't fooled but would play along anyway.

'You're kidding me, Matt.' Clint shook his head. 'Ten days with limited internet contact when we're knee deep in work?'

Matt didn't make the obvious comment to his business partner – the one where he stated the obvious fact that they were always swamped. He'd met the exuberant Texan when they were both doing graduate computer studies at the Massachusetts Institute of Technology and they'd instantly become friends. About six years ago they reconnected when Clint was doing business in Nashville and over a few beers one night they'd confessed a mutual desire to be their own bosses. Within a few months they combined Matt's technical writing genius with Clint's more outgoing personality to create TekSpeak and now had thriving branches in Nashville, Knoxville and Chattanooga. They balanced each other well with Clint happily leaving the bulk of the technical side to Matt while he was relieved to let his friend be the affable face of TekSpeak and take charge of touting for potential business. They were opening in Atlanta in less than two months and Clint had big plans for further expansion including franchising their business model nationally and internationally.

'Would *you* be able to say no to Miss Mary?' He turned the tables on his old friend. They both knew the brash man with his white Stetsons and cowboy boots was as soft-hearted as Matt where it came to his own mother. Last year the slender, white-haired lady welcomed Matt into her home on a visit to Dallas and it'd been obvious where Clint's steely determination came from.

'Heck, no.' Clint slapped Matt's shoulder. 'I'll cover for you but you'd better get Roger on board and up to scratch.' Roger Clements, the new man they'd taken on, was ambitious and Matt wasn't sure of him yet. 'I'm guessin' you're not taking the beautiful Lindsey along.' He teased, referring to the investment banker Matt had gone out with on a couple of recent dates.

'As if.' He never brought girlfriends to meet his mother because it would lead to unsubtle hints of wedding bells and grandchildren. Neither were in his plans for the future.

'Maybe there'll be some cute girl to practise your rusty social skills on.'

Matt laughed. 'Don't be stupid. My sixty-five year old mother will probably be one of the youngest on the tour and I'll be considered a baby. It's aimed at older Americans who want to be able to say they've "done Europe".' Matt was in his element writing a user manual for a complicated smartphone or putting together an online help guide for banking services but people were another story. He'd been a solitary child, but not unhappy. His mother always put the blame on the fact he hadn't had a father's influence rather than her son's naturally introverted personality. He was simply happier with his own company most of the time which was something his outgoing mother found impossible to understand. Being trapped in a coach full of people for ten days would stretch him to breaking point but he'd suck it up for her sake.

Clint pulled out his wallet and tossed a twenty dollar bill on the table. 'This says I'm right and you're wrong. Those cute little ole European girls will be falling all over you.'

Matt threw down a twenty of his own. 'Winner takes all. Like taking candy from a baby.'

Clint perched on the edge of Matt's desk. 'Don't try to trick me either. You're a lousy liar. I'll know.'

Ruefully Matt was forced to admit his friend was right. His mother's insistence on scrupulous honesty made him somewhat of a liability in the business world as well as in his personal life. Women always proclaimed their desire for a truth and integrity in a man but Matt's experience proved otherwise. He took them literally and gave an honest opinion if asked, which was why there'd be no third date with Lindsey. She'd flown into a temper when he told her the new green dress she'd bought *did* make her backside look bigger. Matt never said he found the fact unappealing but she'd screamed at him that it was no wonder he was thirty-eight and single. He had no qualms about taking Clint's bet. He was going on this coach trip to make his mother happy and opening himself up to more humiliating run-ins with the opposite sex wasn't on his agenda.

They shook hands and Matt tried to ignore the satisfied gleam in Clint's bright blue eyes.

Chapter Three

Sarah froze. Any second now Althea would finish paying for her shopping and turn around. Without running out of the shop, which she refused to do, she was trapped. For the last year they'd successfully avoided each other but today their luck had finally run out.

Their friendship had flourished from the first days together in primary school and survived all the usual ups and downs until Althea's huge betrayal broke it into a million pieces. In the pub, over glasses of their favourite chardonnay, her best friend had listened sympathetically to Sarah's concerns about her shaky marriage while conducting a secret affair with Tim. The horror when he asked for a divorce and spelled out the reason would never leave Sarah.

'Oh.' The colour leeched from Althea's face as she registered Sarah's presence. For a second she harboured the uncharitable hope that her ex-friend might faint and knock over the precarious stack of tinned peas next to the counter. 'Hello, Sarah. How are you?'

'I'm fine.' She plastered on the biggest, fakest smile ever as her glance took in the slight baby bump pressing at Althea's skin-tight silky blue top. 'I hear congratulations are in order. I hope you'll be very happy.' The lie tumbled out and the puzzled expression she received in return made it worth every false word. 'I'm sorry I'll miss the big day but I'm going to be touring Europe over Easter.'

'Really?'

Plainly Althea didn't believe her so Sarah needed to come up with something more convincing. 'Yes. Mum and I are meeting up with my new boyfriend so they can get to know each other ... before we take things any further.' The ridiculous story made her blush which Sarah hoped conveyed pleasured embarrassment.

'I'm really happy you're seeing someone. Moving on is healthy.'

Althea's earnestness put murderous thoughts in Sarah's head but she dredged up another sickening smile. 'We're grown-ups.' She shrugged. 'Life's too short.'

'Where's your boyfriend from? How long have you been going out?' The questions kept coming and Sarah wished she had the nerve to confess the truth. She refused to give her old friend the satisfaction so she'd have to make up something and when she got back from holiday let it be known on the village grapevine that things hadn't worked out. Being careful not to give too many details a description of her mythical boyfriend emerged. The holiday brochure had stated that the trip originated in the United States so Sarah seized on that fact and made him American. It'd be much easier to get rid of an imaginary man she'd supposedly met online who came from four thousand miles away than one merely across the Channel.

'He sounds great. If he comes to Cornwall maybe the four of us could get together for a meal?'

What planet was Althea living on? Did she really think it would happen this side of hell freezing over? Sarah murmured a response that could be taken either way and noticed a slight uncertainty in her ex-friend's demeanour as if it'd suddenly occurred to her that she'd been beyond tactless.

'I must be going or Tim will worry.' Althea's voice trailed away and she tentatively reached a hand out towards Sarah.

Quickly sidestepping out of the way she avoided the unwanted contact. Their days of friendly hugs were over and she couldn't imagine the day when they'd ever be welcome again.

'I've come for our pasties.' Sarah called brightly over to Mrs Graham and heard the shop bell ring behind her as her old friend left. Gently exhaling she opened her purse and got out some money. This little episode would be all around the village by morning. More sympathy. Exactly what she didn't need or want.

Matt listened to Roger Clements pontificating on how TekSpeak should go about moving forward and gritted his teeth. The younger man was sharp but that didn't mean he had to like him. He'd caught the gleam of satisfaction in Roger's dark eyes when he discovered he'd be heading up the Atlanta project while Matt was away. Clint would be in charge overall but micromanaging wasn't his style and who knew what the new employee might try to get away with.

'Naturally I'll keep you informed on a daily basis—' Roger's smooth assertion didn't mollify Matt in the least '—although it might be necessary for me to make time-sensitive decisions if your internet connections are of the piece of string variety.' His condescending laughter irritated Matt but he managed to keep on his bland smile. People often underestimated him because he appeared to be quiet and unassuming but when the time was right Roger would discover Matt was no pushover.

There was a lot to be done before he flew out with his mother next Thursday. 'I hope you don't have any plans for tomorrow?' He pinned down Roger, daring him to admit he might not want to work on a Saturday.

'I cleared my schedule for the whole weekend. I was sure we'd have lots to go over.'

Matt's tight nod of acknowledgement was the best he could manage. Inwardly he wondered if this was how terrified parents felt handing their precious child over to a babysitter. He stifled a laugh as he tried to imagine what Roger and Clint would say if they could read his thoughts. Work consumed his life and the image of Matt as a father was ridiculous. He'd been horrified to hear Clint's plans to make his fortune and retire at forty-five to raise rodeo horses on his Texas ranch. Matt couldn't imagine his hardworking friend not chasing the next business opportunity but Clint had sworn he'd be able to switch off without any trouble at all.

'It'll be a different challenge, pal. Gotta give my mama a bunch of grandkids to bounce on her knee. Keep the Jackson name goin'.'

Matt wisely kept his opinion that Clint was mad to himself. No woman would ever change *his* mind.

Chapter Four

For the first time in nearly nine hours Matt could fully stretch out his legs. Thanks to his mother's refusal to let him upgrade their plane tickets his lanky six foot four frame had been wedged into a space more suited to a midget. She'd spent the flight getting to know the half dozen or so other people who they were going to be incarcerated with for the next ten days. Like a well-trained teacher Cecily found out everyone's names, where they came from and all about their families before they even landed in London. As Matt had predicted they were all north of sixty and for most it was their first trip to Europe. He'd kept to himself with his head deep in a computer programming book and his headphones firmly on. The rest of the tour group would meet them in London having flown from other destinations in the States. Kayley, the perky tour guide, had informed them there were also some "genuine Brits" joining them to round out the group.

He glanced around his hotel room and was supremely grateful he'd put his foot down and paid the supplement to get them single rooms on the tour. They had a free afternoon before the ominously named "Speed Date Getalong" at five o'clock. Kayley made it clear, with a swing of her bleached blonde ponytail, that naps to get over jet-lag were the order of the day and everyone had dutifully obliged. Except for Matt. He'd fired up his laptop and checked emails before taking a long, hot shower and changing into fresh clothes. Feeling half-human again he intended to make the most of the sunny spring day and go for a much needed walk.

The lock on the door rattled and Matt heard a woman's sharp voice out in the corridor.

'Why do these stupid things never work?'

More rattling ensued and he guessed he'd better open the door before the interloper kicked it down.

'Looking for someone, ma'am?' Even with her cheeks glowing beet red with embarrassment the young woman glaring at him was well worth a second look. With her cloud of dark hair, pale lightly freckled skin, soft dark brown eyes and a wide, generous mouth she could tempt him into losing any dumb bet.

'I believe you're in the wrong room.'

For a second the crisp British accent knocked him off kilter but he quickly rebounded. 'If I'm in the wrong room why doesn't your key card work, ma'am?'

'This is room 331?'

'Yep. Mind if I take a look?' Matt prised the card from her fingers. 'Easy mistake. Yours is 313.' She snatched it back and stared in disbelief obviously thinking he was an uneducated American who couldn't read his numbers properly.

'Goodness. I am sorry. I'm not usually so ... scatterbrained.' She stumbled over her apology and Matt caught the eye of an older woman hovering behind his would-be room thief. They both started to laugh and Miss Haughty glanced between them with a puzzled expression on her face. For a second he expected to be told off but the corners of her mouth twitched and she joined in their laughter.

Able to laugh at herself. He appreciated that.

'We'd better find our correct room. Mr ...'

'Anderson. Matt Anderson. From Nashville, Tennessee. Music City USA.' He thrust out his hand and shook hers, registering strength, warmth and softness as he held on a shade too long for politeness.

'Sarah Agnoli, from St. Trewin in the wilds of remote Cornwall.'

'Land's End, tin mines and pirates, right?' Her obvious surprise gave him a kick. With a teacher for a mother he'd been well drilled in always being prepared whether it was in his work or play. 'Agnoli's not a very Cornish name.'

'My father was Italian.'

English reserve and Mediterranean passion. An interesting combination. 'By the way I think you'll find it's back down towards the elevator.'

'What is?'

'Your room.' He chuckled as she blushed again, an even deeper, hotter shade of red this time.

Without another word she grabbed her suitcase handle and strode away from him. *Pity.*

The butterflies in Sarah's stomach fluttered as she glanced around the crowded room full of people talking and having a good time. When she'd expressed her reluctance to come to this party her mother said it was because she spent so long with three and four year olds she'd forgotten how to have an adult conversation. Neither of them mentioned the dent in her self-confidence caused by her failed marriage but the spectre of Tim was there all the same. She seized a glass of white wine from a passing waiter and drank it down far too quickly. Spotting her mother in animated conversation with a woman about her own age Sarah sidled behind a small group gathered around the buffet table to make her way over to the bar.

'Found any good hotel rooms recently?'

Sarah groaned. 'Not you again.' The rude response slipped out before she could help it.

'Obviously I made a good impression.'

Matt's quick retort drew a smile out of her. He had no idea. When she'd first heard his warm, honeyed drawl her insides turned to jelly and she'd had to force herself not to behave like a school girl with her first crush. Apart from the brief blip with her overtly good looking ex-husband Sarah was attracted to men who didn't try too hard. Matt Anderson, with his faded jeans, simple grey T-shirt and mop of dark blond wavy hair had shaken her up like a well-mixed martini.

He gestured to the stool next to him. 'You gonna give me a chance to redeem myself?'

'I think I'm the one who needs to do that. You must think I'm an idiot and rude with it.' She preferred to be straightforward. The shrewd way Matt appraised her with his cool, dark blue eyes was disconcerting until his killer smile reappeared making her forcefully aware of the fact Tim hadn't killed off *all* her hormones.

'Not at all.' He hesitated for a second. 'Can I buy you a drink?'

She was pretty sure he'd been going to add something else but simply accepted his offer and left it alone – for now.

'Look at you two!'

Sarah flinched as the tour guide appeared, grinning like a hyperactive monkey. She caught the bewildered expression on Matt's face and guessed he wasn't a fan of Kayley either.

'I was searching for you both and here you've introduced yourselves already.' She pouted. 'You'll put me out of a job.'

Matt's eyebrow rose almost imperceptibly and Sarah struggled to keep her composure.

'The white-haired lady over by the piano is lookin' like jet lag's catchin' up with her. You might want to help her upstairs before she falls over.' Matt pointed across the room.

'Oops. Better go,' Kayley exclaimed and rushed off mere seconds before Sarah collapsed into helpless giggles.

'You're awful.'

'Listen who's talkin'.'

'What on earth are you doing on this tour anyway? You strike me as an unlikely candidate for a race around Europe with a coach full of old-age pensioners.' *In other words what's a gorgeous man like you doing in my orbit? Did I win the lottery and no one told me?*

'Is that what you call them here?' He avoided the question. 'We prefer seniors or the latest fad is "third agers".'

'Maybe we're more honest,' Sarah tossed back at him. 'You still haven't answered me.'

'See the tall, elegant lady dressed in bright orange in the middle of that group?' He gestured towards an attractive woman having a good time as everyone took pictures of each other with their mobile phones. 'That's my mother. This is her retirement gift. A reward for forcing Shakespeare into the heads of apathetic teenagers for the last forty years.'

'And you're a good, dutiful son.' At her words a shadow crossed his face.

'Not really. I'm too busy to do a stellar job most of the time.'

'Busy doing what?' She took a stab. 'You mentioned Nashville so I'll take a guess you're a big country music star I've never heard of and for some reason you've left the boots and cowboy hat behind.'

'You couldn't be further from the truth. Trust me if you ever hear me sing you'll be searching for ear plugs. And my piano lessons ended after a month when the teacher pleaded with my mother to let me stop.'

'I'm tone deaf too so we've something in common. It's a bit of a drawback for a nursery school teacher but luckily the children don't usually notice.' Sarah realised he still hadn't told her what he *did* do for a living. 'So what does occupy all your time in Nashville?'

He drained his beer before setting the glass back on the bar. 'You teachers are all alike. My mother never lets me or her students get away with not answering the question either.'

'Is it a state secret?'

Matt sighed. 'Nope. It's me being dumb. I'm a technical writer which means I'm the geek who writes instruction manuals and online banking instructions. I co-own a business that's doin' okay so I'm kept real busy.'

She guessed he was playing down his success, a plus in her book. Tim's boastful nature had been a bone of contention between them but he could never turn off his habit of "selling" himself to everyone he met. He'd found a soul mate in Althea because her old friend was never one to hide her talents. 'I'm sure you are. People like me desperately need people like you to help us make sense of things.' A tinge of colour darkened his skin and she realised she'd embarrassed him.

'I sure haven't thought of it that way before,' he mumbled.

'My mother's with me too.' Sarah gently changed the subject. 'She's the grey-haired woman in the blue dress over by the fake potted plant.'

'How do you know it's fake?'

'Regular leaves. Unnatural shine. Too symmetrical.' She rattled off the reasons, not adding the fact she'd almost been fooled herself and only found out by touching the plant when they first came in. 'We won this holiday in a competition.' Sarah proceeded to give him all the details. Tim always complained she was a typical teacher who didn't know how to give a brief explanation of anything but Matt didn't appear to be bored and asked all sorts of questions about Cornwall, her job and why they chose this particular tour. He was a good listener and finally she stopped talking and looked over at Matt's mother again. The photo taking session gave her a mad idea. She picked up her wine and drained it in one deep gulp. 'I want to ask you a big favour,' she blurted out and rushed on before she could lose her nerve.

Chapter Five

Was the woman completely mad? Before she made the bizarre suggestion Matt's mind had been running along the lines of saying to heck with Clint's bet and exploring the possibility of a holiday romance with the delectable Sarah. Right now he was doing a rapid rethink.

'You want to take photos of us together around Europe and plaster them all over the internet so your ex-husband and ex-best friend will believe your lie about having a new boyfriend?' He carried on before she could answer. 'Why me?'

'There's no one else here young enough for it to make sense,' she said, staring down at her empty glass as though she wished it would magically refill.

Matt laughed. He couldn't help it. Often he'd complained about women not appreciating his honesty and now he'd found one who was equally truthful. It served him right.

'Sorry. That sounded …'

'Don't bother trying to sugar coat it, sweetheart, it's a lost cause.' He thought hard. This could kill two birds with one proverbial stone. He'd help Sarah on the condition they let Clint into their little agreement. Matt wouldn't be free to date anyone else if Sarah was flooding Facebook with pictures of them at regular intervals. Bet over. Matt picked up her wine glass. 'Another?' She nodded and gave a tentative smile as though she knew he was up to something.

Five minutes later they shook hands. Sarah and

Matt had come to the conclusion that they needed to let their mothers in on their little deceit or they'd drop themselves in no end of trouble. Cecily kept nagging him to date more and Sarah's mother fretted about her failed marriage plus the fact she hadn't been on a date in the last year. It'd give both of them a breathing space and when the ten days were over Matt and Sarah could go their separate ways with no harm done.

Sarah's beautiful smile hit him straight in the gut and a brief flash of regret for what might've been zipped through Matt. She appealed to him far too much but living four thousand miles apart wasn't exactly a recipe for romance. Apart from anything else she was still getting over the failure of her brief marriage to a jerk who'd apparently ditched her for Sarah's best friend.

'Time to start?' He ran a hand over his hair, smoothing down the unruly waves.

'You're sure?'

'We're not harming anyone. They've hurt you enough. Plus you're helping me out too. It's a win-win.'

'Alright.' Her flat tone of voice held none of the enthusiasm of a few minutes ago. Easing her hand away she pulled her phone out of her handbag. 'Would you mind putting your arm around me?'

Matt stifled a smile. 'I don't think that'll be too much of a hardship.' He rested a finger on her mouth and fought down the urge to kiss away her uncertainty. His instant attraction to Sarah was totally unlike his usual cautious behaviour when it came to women and he couldn't work out what exactly brought it on. She was certainly pretty but he'd met far more

24

conventionally beautiful women who did nothing for him. 'You might want to smile. You don't want them to think you're dating a serial killer. You're supposed to make them envious not worried.'

'Sorry.' Big tears filled her eyes and she blinked them away. 'Maybe this is a stupid idea.'

Perversely Matt was more determined now to make this work. 'No. It's not and we're going to see it through. I don't break promises.' He grabbed her phone, threw one arm around her shoulders and ordered her to smile as he took the first picture.

'Sarah, have you tried the cocktail sausages in barbeque sauce? They're really tasty.'

She stared at her mother, now giving Matt a funny look.

'No, but I'm starving.' Sarah almost fell off the stool and only Matt's strong hand grasping her arm saved her from sliding to the ground. 'Show me what's good, Mum.' She practically marched her mother towards the food. Three glasses of wine, an empty stomach and the bizarre interlude with Matt had tied her up in knots. Before she could be interrogated Sarah asked her mother all about the people she'd been speaking to and what she thought of the tour guide.

'I don't know what you're playing at, love, but I'll find out. For now I'll put it down to the wine and excitement.' Betty's sharp comment hung between them and Sarah knew she'd be in trouble later. All because her pride couldn't stand the thought of Althea and Tim feeling sorry for her any longer. 'There are some lovely people in our group.' Her mother pointed to five elderly men in matching bright red shirts chatting

25

loudly up by the bar. 'Those are the BC's. Depending on which one of them you talk to it either refers to the baseball caps they all wear or to their age.' Betty laughed. 'The two very tanned couples sitting near the piano are all from Florida. Well, they're from Canada really but are what they call snowbirds because they migrate south in the winter for the warmer weather.'

Sarah's mind drifted back to Matt. She'd picked up on his innate sense of reserve by the way he held himself apart earlier, sitting at the far end of the bar away from everyone else. Strangely enough he didn't seem to mind talking to her and the teasing smile in his beautiful deep blue eyes intrigued her far more than it should.

'You haven't heard a word I just said.'

'Of course I did,' Sarah protested. 'Tell me more.'

Somehow she survived the rest of the evening and while her mother got ready for bed Sarah finally got up the nerve to look at the photo she'd taken of her and Matt. Studying it objectively she decided their wide smiles would fool anyone and before she could change her mind Sarah altered her Facebook status to "In a relationship" and posted the picture. She sent a text to Matt telling him to do the same and smiled a couple of minutes later when his posting showed up. Sarah and Matt Anderson were now officially a couple.

Super excited to be in London with my Nashville beau!

Sarah tucked into her breakfast and ignored her mother who was giving her the evil eye. Snippets of conversation from the Americans on the next table made her smile. The Snowbirds, as she thought of them, were complaining about the lack of pancakes or waffles in the hotel's breakfast selection and puzzled by the odd bacon, strange baked beans and cooked tomatoes. There was only one other English couple on the tour – Grace and Viola Hawkins, a pair of elderly sisters from Oxford who were being made a fuss of by their reigning academic, an elderly Harvard professor. Rusty Miles was questioning them on every detail of the Inspector Morse stories and bemoaning the fact he wouldn't get to visit Oxford on this trip.

'I had a chat to your "boyfriend's" mother last night.' Sarah caught the disparaging tone in her mother's voice but didn't react. To say Betty was displeased when Sarah explained about the plan she and Matt had agreed to last night was an understatement. 'Cecily was very surprised to see him talking to you at all because he's apparently very clever with computers but a bit of a loner. She despairs of him ever settling down with a good woman and wants to find him a genuine girlfriend not a pretend one …'

Sarah didn't reply and poured them both a fresh cup of tea. The American was the most interesting man she'd met in a long time. *Make that ever.* Matt was good-looking, intelligent and with a quirky sense of humour to match her own. She suspected underneath his outwardly reserved personality was an incredibly sexy man. *Control yourself. Agreeing to have his photo taken occasionally doesn't mean anything more than the fact he feels sorry for you.*

'Do you fancy going on the "Speed Sightsee London in Eight Hours" tour today?' Betty suddenly asked, changing the subject. Why would either of them want

27

to spend a day racing around all the highlights of London that they'd seen so many times before?

'Um, not really.'

'Cecily said it's what they're planning on doing.'

Poor Matt. Being herded around the Tower of London, Buckingham Palace, Westminster Abbey and a half dozen other un-missable spots would be an endurance test for anyone. 'Do *you* want to go?'

'It might be fun. Neither of us have done the touristy places for a long time. It'd be interesting to see it through the eyes of people who've never been there.'

Sarah refused to rise to the bait being dangled in front of her and managed to smile and agree. Inwardly she said goodbye to the quiet wander around the National Portrait Gallery and lunchtime concert at St Martin-in-the-Fields church she'd mentally had planned.

'Good. Let's go and get ready. The coach leaves at nine.' Betty jumped up and headed for the door, leaving Sarah to trail along in her wake.

Half way through the day Sarah stood on the pavement outside Madame Tussauds waiting for her mother to join her and wondering if she could survive another five hours of Kayley's relentlessly upbeat commentary on the joys of London.

'Photo time?'

She jerked around to face Matt, grim-faced and miserable. 'Are you having fun yet?'

'Oh, yeah. My idea of a good day.' He winced. 'Shit. My mother's spotted us. I told her about your mad scheme and—'.

'Don't tell me – she hated it. Mine did too.'

Matt shrugged. 'I told her politely to mind her own business.'

'Thanks. I'm sorry if I've caused you any trouble.'

'She's been bending my ear all morning about what a great person your mother is and you're apparently one step short of being a saint. Anyone would think *I* was the one taking advantage of *you*.'

'Oh, dear. If it's any consolation I'm hardly a saint. From what I've seen you don't fit your mother's description of a computer nerd who's a bit of a loner and useless around women either so I think we're even.'

'Ritual humiliation by mom. Nothin' quite like it.' His smile faded and Sarah didn't know what to say next. Perhaps Cecily's summing up was more accurate than he cared to admit.

Sarah pulled out her phone. 'How about I take a picture of you on your own? Could you manage to gaze adoringly at me?'

He pulled an ugly face and stuck out his tongue. 'Will that work?'

She smacked his arm. 'Behave.' The instant he laughed the years dropped from Matt's lean, austere features. Snap. Check photo. Add caption. Post.

Am I a lucky girl, or what?!!!!!

Sarah slipped her phone back in her bag.

'Thanks,' Matt murmured.

'What for?' As she met his gaze Sarah couldn't help staring into his mesmerising blue eyes. For a few wonderful seconds the rest of the world fell away and nothing else existed but her and this intriguing man.

He lifted his hand to her cheek and stroked his

warm fingers over her skin sending a rush of heat up her neck to flood her face. 'Not letting me be a jerk.'

'You're welcome,' she croaked. Sarah needed to walk away before she made even more of a fool of herself. Nothing about this was going according to plan.

Chapter Six

'It sure is a pretty day for a drive through the countryside.' Cecily settled into her seat by the window and got out the guide book she hadn't been without since they left Nashville. If anyone was going to get the most out of this trip it'd be his mother. 'By the way I expect to be introduced to your cute little English rose today, Matt. Or am I supposed to call her your "girlfriend"?'

They were heading to Dover where they'd cross the Channel over to Calais, drive a couple of hours to Brussels and get a swift tour around the city before reaching their hotel. In other words they'd only escape from the bus when they were being fed and watered. Matt was interested to observe how people had already separated into smaller groups of like-minded individuals and decided it'd provide perfect research material for any anthropologist. He realised his mother was still talking.

'I said …'

'I heard. She's not *my* anything . You know that.' He insisted. A phone was thrust in his face with the picture of the two of them smiling into the camera.

'Really? You could fool me. She's a pretty girl. You'd make a good couple.'

He'd had several teasing emails from Clint after he'd told his friend about his agreement with Sarah. Mostly on the lines of how cute she was and why was he being a dumbass.

'I'll introduce you. Okay?' He slumped back

in his seat and closed his eyes to put a stop to the interrogation. Matt wished he'd heard from Roger before having to shut down his laptop after breakfast. The only update he'd got so far on the Atlanta opening hadn't been very satisfactory.

A couple of hours later he discovered his tough mother had her vulnerable side as he passed her another sick bag. His reassurance that it was only a ninety-minute ferry ride was met with a ripe curse he'd never before heard pass her lips.

Matt wandered out on deck and zipped up his old leather jacket against the blustery wind buffeting the ferry.

'That's one more thing I've found out about my imaginary boyfriend.' Sarah's cheerful voice interrupted his thoughts and he swung around to face her. 'You're a good sailor.'

She really was a beauty although he guessed she'd call him stupid if he told her so. Matt wasn't an expert on women – his mother was right there – but he wasn't as clueless as she thought either. Everything about Sarah glowed with life and that beat everything in his books. Matt was pretty damn sure her ex-husband was an idiot to have let her go. *He* certainly wouldn't do if … He pulled himself back to reality. 'Right back at you. How's your mom?'

Sarah scrunched up her nose. 'Sitting perfectly still down below and planning to stay fixed in position until we land. If she moves she swears she'll be ill. What about yours?'

'Sick as a dog and hating me for being an insensitive son.' Matt chuckled. 'Think I should go and tell her France is in sight?'

'Maybe not.' Sarah shivered and instinctively he slipped his arm around her, feeling absurdly pleased when she made no effort to pull away. A drift of delicate floral perfume teased his nostrils and Matt fought to remember this was all make believe.

'Selfie time again?' He abruptly suggested, dropping his hand back down by his side. Sarah looked puzzled and if he hadn't been certain of her feelings towards him Matt might have thought she was disappointed.

Great excuse for a warm cuddle on the cold and windy ferry to France!

'Have you travelled outside of America much before this?' Sarah closed up her phone. When he'd wrapped his arms around her and she'd nestled against his soft black leather jacket it'd taken every ounce of restraint she possessed not to kiss him.

'Only on business.' Matt explained he'd travelled the world working on short-term projects for a wide range of businesses using his technical writing skills before starting his own business. 'I go in, get the job done and get out as fast as possible. I'm dealing with similar people to me – tech geeks – so we don't waste time on socialising none of us enjoy.'

She couldn't imagine wasting the opportunity to sightsee and get a sample of different cultures but kept her opinion to herself. Matt's enthusiasm for his work was evident but he didn't appear to have any outside life and Sarah wondered how anyone could exist that way. She loved her job but equally enjoyed going out with friends, helping backstage with the local pantomime and taking long walks along the beautiful Cornish coastline.

'You agree with my mother, don't you?' he challenged.

'She considers me a sad workaholic. What's wrong with focusing all your energy on something you love doing?' Before she could consider how to reply without hurting his feelings Matt shoved his hands in his pockets and shrugged. 'Forget it. Doesn't matter. See you in Brussels for another photo op.' He strode away across the deck and disappeared down the stairs out of sight.

In Matt's behaviour she saw echoes of three-year-old Justin Warner who'd joined her class after Christmas. Being an only child, bigger than the other boys, and very clever, Justin's self-contained confidence put the other children off. He'd acted as though he didn't care about having any friends but deep down she'd guessed he wanted nothing more than to fit in. She paired him up with Maddie Ryan who was the youngest of six children with a naturally sunny disposition. The little girl struggled with a speech impediment and Justin immediately started to help her learn her alphabet. In response the other children thawed towards him and he opened up. Was it arrogant to think she could help Matt the same way and be his Maddie? Probably. There was no reason to think he wanted to be different. *Yes. There is. You saw his stony expression when he described himself through his mother's eyes.*

She'd give it more thought. Sarah couldn't bounce ideas off her mother as she usually did because they weren't on the same page for once when it came to her pretend relationship with Matt. For now she'd look forward to Brussels because she wasn't going to waste a minute of this unexpected holiday worrying about *any* man. *Liar. You already have. Witness the social media photo blitz.* Who was she fooling?

* * *

34

It was her turn for the window seat and Sarah kept her nose pressed against the glass all the way around Brussels. She was entranced by the medieval city and soaked in the wonderful architecture as they drove around the superb Grand Place square with its ornate baroque houses and Town Hall. Her only complaint came from not being able to get out and see it the way she'd enjoy far more – on foot. This would definitely go on her list of places to return to one day. Finally they were allowed to shake off the confines of the bus to see the famous Manneken Pis statue of a boy peeing into a fountain up close.

'Well built young man isn't he?' Matt's rumbling laughter right behind her startled Sarah and she stepped back on his foot, making her stumble and nearly fall over. 'Careful there.' His firm hand on her arm steadied her. 'This little fellow should come and join our scandalous Musica statue in downtown Nashville. It's a bunch of naked dancers frolicking around known as "The Nekkid People". He'd be right at home.' Sarah couldn't resist laughing along with him and bathed in the unself-conscious good humour he often revealed around her. 'People dress our statue up sometimes and I hear this one has a whole exhibit of costumes in a museum. They could swap clothes.'

She bit her tongue on the joke she'd been about to make about taking his photo alongside the statue for comparison.

'Not with my mama watching, Ms Sarah.' Matt's eyes shone and he waved a warning finger in the air. 'And here was me thinkin' you're a proper English lady.'

'How boring.'

'Oh, I don't find you the least bit boring.'

'You don't know me.' Sarah's cheeks flamed.

'I sure would like to.'

They stared at each other in shock. Innuendo laced flirting definitely wasn't part of their agreement but they'd slipped into it as easily as if they'd been a real couple.

'If my son is too bad-mannered to introduce us I'll do it myself.'

Sarah startled as a hand was thrust at her and she turned around to meet Cecily Anderson's curiosity head on. This woman clearly didn't know the meaning of the word shy and her piercing emerald eyes missed nothing as they went through the normal pleasantries.

'I think this fake Facebook thing you're up to is a load of nonsense but he won't listen to me. It's a pity because you could be real good for my boy,' Cecily declared, and fixed her steely gaze back on Matt who plainly wished he could vaporise on the spot. 'Enjoy yourselves.' She strode off, calling out to one of her new friends as she walked back towards the coach.

Sarah and Matt stared awkwardly at each other again and she tried to think of something to say that wasn't completely vacuous. Suddenly the Star Wars theme music jangled and Matt yanked his phone from his jeans pocket to glare at the screen.

'Sorry. Gotta get this.'

She nodded and wandered off to leave him in peace. If she survived the next week unscathed Sarah was never going to lie again.

Chapter Seven

Matt wasn't pleasing anyone today. He'd pulled out of the Rhine River cruise and declared his intention to go ahead by train to the hotel in Frankfurt where they were due to spend the night. To say his mother wasn't happy was an understatement. She'd given him the silent treatment over breakfast and made pointed comments to the other people at their table. Being a social outcast wasn't a new experience but today it'd needled him. The fact that the reputation of TekSpeak was at stake and he could lose a significant amount of money meant nothing stacked against his mother's annoyance. He'd promised to make it up to her tomorrow but she'd only scoffed and turned away.

Add in the unsatisfactory phone call with Roger back in Atlanta and the day was going downhill fast. Matt had finally gotten hold of the other man after days of trying and although Roger's answers weren't outright lies nor were they anything resembling the whole truth. Contracts hadn't been issued to several of the technical writers he'd hand selected to start up the new office because Roger had taken on unknown people at cheaper rates. From the beginning Matt and Clint differentiated themselves from other similar firms by only employing the best and brightest and paying them well enough so that they rarely left to work elsewhere. He wasn't happy to find Clint sitting back and letting their new employee ride roughshod over their business principles.

Added to all that was Sarah and the whole

convoluted mess they'd got themselves into. On the ferry she'd slipped into his arms so naturally and yesterday in Brussels he'd been within seconds of kissing her until his mother's interference saved him. First thing this morning he'd texted her his plans for the day and received an instant reply saying she was sorry and would miss him. Matt couldn't get her out of his mind even when he tried. As soon as he arrived at his hotel room today he'd walked out onto the small balcony and been on the verge of suggesting it'd make a good photo when he'd realised she wasn't with him. The woman was under his skin whether he liked it or not.

Against her will Sarah found herself sympathising with Matt. Even she, who liked being around people, was starting to feel claustrophobic. It might only be a six-hour cruise but the guide giving the running commentary was a German version of the infamous Kayley and grated on Sarah's good nature. Throw in copious amounts of free wine and two interfering mothers taking advantage of Matt's absence to pester her non-stop and Sarah's day sucked. The grey skies and constant drizzle made the supposedly beautiful Rhine River resemble anywhere else in the world when it rained. The medieval castles and pretty towns might as well have been Scotland or France for all she could make out through the heavy mist.

Sneaking up on the top deck she pulled on her waterproof jacket and found a quiet spot out of sight. Sarah perched on an empty bench and checked her phone for a signal.

Hallelujah. She tapped in a quick message and

waited, hoping against hope that Matt wouldn't be so engrossed in work he'd ignore her.

Sorry. Busy. See you later.

Sarah read his brusque reply, swore and threw her phone back in her bag. *Fine. Be that way. Remember he's not a real boyfriend. Being sympathetic and there for you wasn't part of the agreement.* She hated the fact her conscience made complete sense.

'There you are. Thank goodness.' Betty appeared on deck, her face pale and drawn. 'Kayley was doing a head count and couldn't find you.

'I'm surprised she can manage the maths.'

'Sarah! It's not like you to be unkind. She's a sweet girl.' Betty launched into the whole background story of the guide who'd apparently overcome a terrible family life, childhood illness and dyslexia to get where she was today.

'Sorry,' she mumbled and plastered on a bright smile. 'Let's go and reassure Kayley that the Lorelei Rock siren didn't tempt me into the icy waters,' she joked about the notorious spirit who was supposed to lure sailors to their death from her rocky outpost on the river.

'Cecily texted Matt to see if he might join us at Rüdesheim for the wine tasting.' *Good luck. I'll bet you ten pounds the answer is no.* 'He hasn't replied but it would be nice, wouldn't it?'

Sarah made a non-committal answer and carried on walking.

'He's a nice man. Quiet, but there's nothing wrong with that. Your father was a thoughtful man.'

Please give up, Mum.

'Cecily's sure he's worried about problems at work.'

Sarah chose her words with care. 'He has his own business. It's a big responsibility.'

'Cecily was hoping you two might …'

'Then she shouldn't.' Sarah's firm tone of voice made her mother stop dead at the top of the stairs. 'We're friends. Nothing more. Please don't take offense but apart from the whole Facebook picture thing it's nice for me to have some younger company. It's never going to turn into anything more serious.' That was the closest she could come to being honest. It left out the unsettling fact that her feelings for him were deepening and she was on track to being hurt again if she didn't watch out.

'What a pity.' Betty shook her head and grabbed the handrail to go back down below deck. She left Sarah wondering.

The combination of the loud oom-pah band and too many glasses of sweet German wine on an empty stomach gave Sarah a dull headache and she slipped out of the restaurant's side door in search of fresh air. Hopefully the dutiful Kayley wouldn't decide to count her charges again because being forced to explain herself twice in one day would be excessive. Dinner would be served in a few minutes and afterwards they'd get back on the coach for the short drive to Frankfurt.

Idly she checked her phone. Her photo from the ferry yesterday garnered more comments than usual and her heart did a flip when she saw one from Tim.

You make a great couple. Have fun.

She scrolled back through and saw that he and Althea had 'liked' all her recent posts. There was an odd emptiness in the pit of her stomach. She was still divorced. Her ex-husband was still going to marry her ex-best friend soon and have a baby. Nothing had changed. If all this planning and scheming didn't at least make her feel better what was the point? When she saw Matt later she'd call the whole thing off, stop the photo nonsense and go back to enjoying the holiday with her mum as planned.

Her phone beeped.

Romantic moon tonight. Perfect background for jealousy making photo! See you soon to 'enjoy' it together. Matt.

She sighed. Maybe she'd put off telling him until tomorrow. It'd been a long day and she'd missed him.

Perfect. Just going to eat a plate of hearty German food.

Sauerkraut breath doesn't do it for me.

Considering there's no kissing in our agreement it doesn't matter.

Spoilsport.

Why did he keep doing this? Teasing hints of the fun, sexy man Matt kept buried made her want things she couldn't have. Namely him.

I'm tired. Need an early night. Tomorrow is the Romantic Road. We'll save ourselves for that.

She turned off her phone. That way she could fantasise he'd tried to change her mind.

Chapter Eight

'Are you ready for a day of over-the-top German charm being forced down your throat?' Matt asked and wanted to bite off his tongue as Sarah's smile faded. He'd spotted her at the breakfast buffet and waited until she chose a table over by the window before filling his own plate and going to join her.

'I suppose it didn't occur to you that I might actually be looking forward to it?' She sounded puzzled rather than angry. 'I'm well aware that the Romantic Road was a modern invention to lure tourists into the area after the war and I also know we won't have time to see more than the highlights, but frankly I don't care.' Sarah's bright determination made him feel a complete heel. 'You might get to travel with your work – although I don't get the impression you get any pleasure from it – but I don't. My job isn't well paid and since my divorce my holidays are usually spent doing extra tutoring jobs to earn a little more money. Winning this trip was a wonderful surprise.'

'I'm sorry. I didn't mean to …'

She snapped the croissant she was holding in half and threw it back on her plate. Sarah launched into him, holding nothing back. He was thoughtless, arrogant and considered himself superior to everyone else. And those were the least of his faults. She did concede he could be agreeable when he put his mind to it and admitted she enjoyed his sense of humour, but neither made up for what she called his bleak and narrow outlook on life. 'Do you actually get pleasure from anything outside of your computers?'

Yeah, watching you get fired up. Your smile. The way your eyes sometimes soften and glow when you look at me. He said nothing.

'Sorry I'm late, dear.' Betty Agnoli appeared, carrying her breakfast, and Matt jumped up to pull out a chair for her. 'Thank you, Mr Anderson.'

'Call me Matt, please.' Her quick glance between the two of them told him she guessed they'd been arguing. 'Are you looking forward to today's trip, ma'am?'

'Very much and I know my girl can't wait to see the castle with the long name. She'll tell me off for saying so but she's never grown out of fairytales. I think she still imagines herself as Sleeping Beauty.' She laughed and he couldn't help joining in, despite Sarah's obvious mortification.

'She sure is pretty enough to be a princess and any prince lucky enough to kiss her awake would be a fortunate man.' Both women stared at him as though he'd grown two heads. Betty obviously recognised his natural diffidence and was bewildered by his overtly flirtatious comment and Sarah couldn't believe what she was hearing after their recent set-to. He couldn't believe his behaviour either. What on earth was the woman doing to him?

'Is there room for one more?'

Matt groaned under his breath. His mother joining in was exactly what he didn't need. Talk about too many cooks stirring the pot.

'Of course, Cecily.' Betty gestured to the chair next to her and Matt slumped back in his seat as his fate was sealed.

If she was a nicer person Sarah would feel sorry for

him but Matt brought all this on himself and she was tired of always being 'nice'. Being more suspicious of people and not quite as trusting could've made the difference between getting out of her marriage with her dignity intact instead of being trodden on like the proverbial doormat. All Tim had to do was turn on the charm, swear there was a good explanation for his absences and strange phone calls and she'd believed every word. She still wasn't sure what'd brought on her earlier outburst but didn't regret a word.

She sneaked a glance at Matt and was amused to see him shovelling in scrambled eggs as though his life depended on it. Stirring things up more wouldn't be kind but Sarah flashed Cecily her brightest smile. 'I hope you're not going to be neglected again today?' She sensed Matt's eyes boring into her but refused to look his way.

'I'd better not be.' Cecily's schoolteacher tone of voice was uncompromising. 'Even *my* son wouldn't dare to spoil my birthday. I'm sure he has something special planned for tonight.'

'Happy Birthday!' Sarah exclaimed, catching Matt's surge of panic out of the corner of her eye. 'I'm sure he won't let you down.' *Again*. The unspoken word hung in the air, but they all heard it clearly.

'I promise I won't complain about a single thing today and I'm turning my phone off,' Matt insisted. 'No checking on work until we get to Innsbruck tonight after we've enjoyed your birthday treat, mother. You're goin' to love it. I promise.'

He's good. If she didn't know better she'd almost be fooled. By Cecily's stern demeanour Sarah guessed his mother didn't believe for a second that he'd remembered the date or made any plans.

'I'm goin' to love you and leave you, ladies. See you on the bus.' Matt jumped up and hurried away.

'He's off to find me a birthday card and order a dozen red roses to be delivered to the hotel tonight. No doubt he'll collar the guide and get her to organise a cake.' Cecily sighed. 'Imagination was never Matt's strong point. Still, he's a good boy really. I shouldn't complain.' Her eyes twinkled. 'I do of course but he puts up with it.'

It really was none of her business and she should stay out of it but Sarah couldn't resist. 'If you'll excuse me I need to go and brush my teeth before we leave. See you both later.' Leaving Betty and Cecily together probably wasn't a good idea but she was foolish enough to want to help Matt get back into his mother's good books.

Matt jerked open his door. 'What do … Oh, it's you.' Sarah was the last person he'd expected to see and now he'd been rude – again. 'No key card fight today?' A tentative smile crept over her face. 'Do you want to come in?'

'Um, I suppose so.'

'Is it photo time again?' He stepped back to let her enter. 'The view from the balcony's pretty damn impressive.'

'That's not what I'm here for. I thought you might want some help with your mother's birthday.'

He ached to kiss her for being such a sweetheart but wasn't a complete moron. She made it clear last night that kissing wasn't on their agenda. 'How did you guess?'

'That you'd forgotten?' She laughed. 'It was obvious and your poor mother knew it too.'

'Busted.' Matt dangled his head in fake shame and glanced up at her, registering her pink cheeks and the hint of laughter tugging at the corners of her mouth. His sense of humour was supposedly one of his few virtues so he'd milk it for all it was worth. *Why? She's too good for a quick fling and you don't want more. Remember?*

Sarah glanced at her watch and frowned. 'We don't have long.' Her eyes sparkled with mischief. 'I don't want Kayley to call the police and report me missing if I'm not in my assigned seat on the bus.'

'Is that likely?'

'I forget you don't know about yesterday.' She laughed and flopped down into the nearest chair. Matt perched on the arm of the sofa next to her and didn't say a word about the birthday plans, preferring to bask in Sarah's relaxed happiness. 'Our illustrious guide almost had them dredging the Rhine River for me.'

'I guessed the cruise would be boring but I thought you'd manage to handle it without resorting to drastic measures. Did you miss my scintillating company?' Sarah's smile faltered. 'Don't answer in case you incriminate yourself.' He teased but she didn't laugh.

'Did your business problem sort itself out?'

The change of topic threw him for a few seconds. 'Not really.'

'You wish you were back in Nashville.'

'Yeah.' Matt nodded. 'Atlanta really. We're opening a new branch there.' Before he knew what he was doing Matt found himself pouring out to Sarah about all the trouble he was having with Roger Clements. Talking things through helped sort it in his head and on impulse he leaned over and kissed her forehead. The brief touch of her soft, warm skin made Matt shiver and it killed him to pull away. 'Sorry, I know that kiss was against the rules but thanks.'

'What for?' Her breathy voice hinted that she wasn't as indifferent to him as she pretended to be. The knowledge gave Matt hope although he didn't dare ask himself what exactly he was hoping for.

'Listening.'

'Aren't Southern girls good listeners?'

'Not sure.' Matt shrugged. 'I don't date much.' His admission stopped the conversation dead. 'Hey. This isn't getting anything sorted for the birthday girl.' Avoiding her curious gaze he got up and walked over to the table where he'd set up his laptop. *Play along. Please.*

'Much as I hate to suggest it you need to get Kayley in on this.' Sarah's brisk declaration should've made him thankful, but deep down he wished she hadn't let him get away with being his usual buttoned up self. 'Your mother's not shy. She'll like it if they make a fuss of her tonight.' A drift of perfume teased his resolve as she came to stand by him. He'd bet his life she smelled wonderful all over. 'You're very different. What was your father like?'

Matt swallowed hard. Beyond mentioning the fact his father died he'd given Sarah no details. He never did to anyone. 'No clue.' A loud banging on the door interrupted anything he might've considered adding.

'Mr Anderson.'

He'd never been grateful to hear Kayley's shrill voice before, but he was now.

Chapter Nine

Sarah cursed under her breath as Matt hurried to answer the door. She suspected he'd come close to revealing something about his father but now it would be hopeless. Any chance of a private conversation on a coach trip surrounded by fifty-eight inquisitive people was impossible.

'Tut, tut, you two.' Kayley wagged a finger at them both and giggled. 'Your mothers guessed I'd find you here. On the bus please in five minutes or we'll go without you.'

Great idea.

'Hang on a sec please. I need your help.' Matt's tempting drawl had the same effect on the guide as it always did on Sarah judging by Kayley's flushed cheeks. Of course he was totally oblivious because it would never occur to him to turn on his natural, low-key charm on purpose. 'It's my mom's birthday and she deserves better than the routine flowers and card I usually manage.'

'Aren't you the sweetest man.'

Sarah didn't dare look at Matt because they'd be unable to avoid laughing at the poor girl.

Kayley patted his arm. 'Don't you fret. I'll come up with some ideas and run them by you while we're out today.' She flashed a conspiratorial smile over at Sarah. 'Don't worry. I won't tell anyone about you lovebirds.' Skipping happily away she disappeared down the corridor and Matt let out a heavy groan as he slammed the door.

'Wonderful. This is all we need. I must've been stupid to agree to your crazy plan. She'll have us married off before we get to Paris.'

'Excuse me for offering to help. I'll leave you to Kayley's tender mercies.' Sarah snatched up her handbag.

'I didn't mean …'

'You never do.' She snapped and elbowed past him. 'I expect at least two photos today to make up for yesterday. You made an agreement and I expect you to stick to it.' Sarah left Matt with his mouth gaping open. She headed downstairs and discovered her mother was already on the bus, not in their usual seat but sitting towards the front with Matt's mother.

'Cecily's got this guide book with everywhere we're going today and she's going to tell me all about it,' Betty said. 'You don't mind, do you, dear?'

What could she say? No, because I don't want to be stuck with your new friend's rude son all day? Sarah dredged up what she hoped was a convincing smile and assured her mother it wasn't a problem. As she walked away she glanced back over her shoulder to catch them whispering and giggling like schoolgirls. *Be a bit more obvious why don't you? We know you're both desperate to pair us off but it's not going to happen.* This was all her fault.

Before he could arrive and cause a fuss about their seating arrangements she hurried back to her seat and settled in by the window. Sarah kept a close watch on the main door of the hotel and at the last minute Matt sprinted out to the bus, apologising profusely to Kayley as he leapt up the steps. She peeped over the top of her guide book in time to see his gaze sweep over their mothers and light on her. She pretended to be engrossed and Matt's features settled into a grim smile as he made his way down the aisle towards her.

Without a word he wedged himself into the seat next to Sarah and fastened his seat belt. Matt kept his eyes fixed on the seat back in front of him and steeled himself not to react as their arms and thighs brushed in the narrow confines. The first part of the drive was tedious but once they got onto the Romantic Road at Würzburg the beautiful Bavarian countryside drew him in. He wanted to apologise for the way he'd spoken at the hotel but with Sarah's back firmly towards him she wasn't making it easy. *Why should she? You were an idiot.* As they started to drive through the small village of Bad Mergentheim he broke the silence. 'Quite something isn't it?'

She half-turned but didn't smile. 'Don't tell me medieval houses and cobblestone streets are more interesting than a computer screen?'

They are today because you're here to share it with me. 'Can't I enjoy both? I don't ask you if they're more interesting than your students.'

'I'm sorry.' Sarah frowned. 'I tend to be too black and white. My only excuse is that it comes from working with children. They need firm rules and boundaries so they understand what's acceptable behaviour.'

'I sure am sorry you don't always find mine acceptable.' Taking a big chance Matt rested his hand on her shoulder. 'How about we call a truce and enjoy the day?' The warmth crept back into her eyes. 'You want to be my teacher?' he jested. Sarah nodded and turned her attention back to the scenery they were passing. She quietly launched into the history of the area and he didn't let on that his mother bored him to death last night with every single detail of the over two hundred mile route they were tackling today. Sarah's enthusiasm was intoxicating and he didn't intend to spoil the moment. They did better when he kept his mouth shut.

'We'll be in Weikersheim soon. There's a half-hour stop built into the schedule. Long enough to get everyone off for a toilet break and loaded back on again but no chance of seeing the beautiful Renaissance palace, the church or the wine making museum.'

Matt almost said he'd be happy to bring her back one day and see everything she wanted but merely smiled. 'Maybe we can sneak a quick cup of coffee somewhere.'

'You've forgotten our mothers.'

I wish.

'Naughty.' She remonstrated, but he sensed it was automatic rather than a genuine desire to tell him off. 'We could invite them to join us.' When he didn't respond she tapped his arm. 'Very uncharitable, Mr Anderson.'

'Honest, Ms Agnoli.'

She peered at him. 'You are, aren't you?'

He wasn't sure how to respond because she'd made it sound to his detriment, which was confusing. Matt had begun to think she wasn't like all the other women he'd come across who said one thing and meant another.

'It's a compliment. I learned from my disastrous marriage that nothing is more important.' She hesitated for a second. 'Tim's version of the truth was

51

whatever suited him at the time. Once I realised that I still fought to hold onto our marriage because we'd made a commitment to each other and … I didn't take it lightly.'

'He did?'

Sarah went quiet. 'Yes, in my opinion. He might not agree. Tim is very good at making excuses and usually gets away with it.' She exhaled a heavy sigh. 'I only hope he treats Althea better. With the baby coming she has a lot more at stake than I ever did.'

'You're a good person to say that and mean it.' Matt held her gaze and something shifted between them leaving a new sense of understanding. He wasn't sure what to do with it and for now he'd tuck the idea away to be considered later the way he did most things – logically and with all the facts at his disposal.

'I couldn't have said that until very recently but life's too short to waste on being bitter.'

He became aware the coach was slowing down and next thing it'd stopped in the middle of a picturesque small town.

Kayley clapped her hands. 'Thirty minutes. We'll be making a longer stop in Rothenburg very soon so don't make me have to chase anyone back on the bus.'

'Might be worth being late to watch her try,' Matt whispered in Sarah's ear and she buried her head in his chest to stifle her laughter. He couldn't resist holding her for a few wonderful moments. 'I suppose we'd better obey orders.' Reluctantly he eased away.

Ten minutes later they were seated at a sunny table near the ornate baroque church and well out of view of anyone who might be looking for them. He caught her surprise as he ordered their coffees and two of the local specialty pastries in fluent German.

'Another hidden talent?'

Matt shrugged. 'It's helpful for business. I can get by in French and Italian too. My Spanish is shaky but I'm working on it.'

The waiter returned with their order and Sarah's eyes widened.

'Oh, goodness, what on earth is it?'

He'd have to thank his mother later. In the middle of her recitation about Count Wolfgang of Hohenlohe and the Weikersheim Palace she'd mentioned the sweet delicacy known as Schneeballen, or snowballs. Made of strips of pastry wound around a special tool to give them the correct shape and then deep-fried, these had been made in the local area for over three hundred years. Matt was always impressed by traditions that'd been going on for longer than his own country existed. He told Sarah the whole story and she cautiously broke off a piece of the culinary snowball before taking a nibble.

'I chose the traditional style with powdered sugar but they also make them covered in chocolate or nuts and some are stuffed with almond paste.'

She smiled and leaned across the table to brush sugar from his cheek. 'You don't want to leave any visible evidence of our indiscretion.' Sarah blushed, realising the implication that could be read into her words. 'We call this icing sugar.'

'Powdered makes more sense.'

Sarah glanced at her watch. 'How about we take a quick photo before Kayley sends out the bloodhounds?'

This had been a brief indulgence and he wasn't a man to fool himself. She'd nicely reminded him, because she did everything kindly, that this was a set-up nothing more. Matt pulled his chair over next to hers, draped his arm around her shoulder and gave a loving smile as she took a selfie of them together in the sunshine.

Snowballs in April. The best kind. Sweet pastries with my sweetie.

Chapter Ten

Sarah linked arms with her mother as they walked around the centre of Rothenburg.

'It seems odd buying Christmas decorations in April.' Betty picked up a carved wooden nativity scene ornament. They'd decided to save her mother's knees and not walk around the walls of the medieval town but satisfy their urge to shop instead. 'You're looking nice today, dear.'

Normally Sarah chose quiet colours but no one could call her new bright pink jumper tame. 'You don't think it's a bit … much?'

'Not at all and Cecily agreed.'

Knowing she and her wardrobe had been a topic of conversation wasn't what Sarah wanted to hear.

'Did Matt say he liked it?'

Be a bit blunter. Please. 'Why on earth would he?'

'No reason.' Her mother smiled and picked up another Christmas ball. Mentioning Matt had plainly steered the conversation in the direction Betty had been aiming for from the time they got off the coach. 'You keep telling me you and Matt are only friends but Cecily showed me a lot of your photos on her phone today.' Her mother set down the shiny silver ball and fixed her attention on Sarah. 'The way you look at each other seems genuine to me.'

Sarah paid close attention to a miniature gold filigree Christmas tree. 'We're both good at acting. It's only a bit of fun.'

'Really. I still can't understand why you're doing this. I've never considered you to be petty.'

Her mother's comment made her feel small.

'Tim's not worth it. He never was. Oh, he's not a bad man but I never thought he was good enough for you. He and Althea deserve each other.'

She couldn't believe what she was hearing. During all the time she'd gone out with Tim and through their engagement and brief marriage her mother never hinted at having any reservations.

'I still can't believe sometimes what they did. Althea always thought Tim was good-looking, but most women do so that doesn't mean much? He's always been a flirt but there's a long stretch from that to …' She shook her head. 'How on earth did they get away with it? Usually these kind of stories race around the village in no time but I never suspected a thing until the day he asked for a divorce.'

Her mother went oddly quiet and Sarah noticed her fingers trembling. An icy chill trickled down her spine. 'Oh my God. Please tell me I'm being ridiculous to even think this. Did you know they were cheating on me?' The buzz of people around them faded away.

'This isn't the place, dear.' Betty murmured, not able to meet her eyes.

'How could you?'

'I didn't say …'

'You don't need to,' Sarah yelled and stormed out of the shop. She ran across the square and headed for one of the narrow lanes packed with tourists where she could lose herself in the crowd. She pushed her way through, brushing away tears so she could see where she was going. They were due to leave again in an hour and she didn't see how she could go back and pretend everything was alright.

Matt left his mother to explore the Rothenburg Vaults on her own and returned to the bus. She'd have an hour to immerse herself in the displays of costumes and weapons connected to the Thirty Years War, something she'd find fascinating and he'd have simply endured. Kayley opened the coach door and seized on him with glee.

'Come here. I want to tell you what I've got set up for your sweet mom's birthday.' She pulled him up the steps and Matt listened in horror as she described the medieval style dinner she'd organised. There would be period costumes for everyone to wear, a jester and a local music group who specialised in Renaissance music. The idea of being forced into a velvet tunic and tights brought him out in a cold sweat.

'Wonderful. You've done a great job,' he lied through gritted teeth. Matt's acting abilities stretched to the utmost as he pretended enthusiasm for the festivities looming over the day. 'If you won't think me rude I'm goin' to check my phone while my mom's busy.' Kayley, a phone addict herself, nodded vigorously and shooed him away.

Slumping in the seat he briefly closed his eyes and thought about Sarah. *Bad idea*. She'd looked adorable today. Matt was no fashion guru but the bright pink thing she'd worn brought out the colour in her fair skin and the low-scooped neckline hinted at curves she usually kept well under wraps. He had no objection to jeans and T-shirts, they were his usual go to as well, but still looked forward to seeing her in costume tonight.

Matt pictured her in a figure hugging medieval dress, maybe in a rich dark green velvet, something he could run his hands over while they danced. *Stop the pipe dream, idiot. She's using you to get back at her ex-husband and keep her mother off her case. And you're no better.*

Matt turned on his phone. Daydreaming was for losers. He checked his messages and groaned when he read the succession of texts from Clint. Things were going from bad to worse at TekSpeak. He ought to get on the next plane back to Nashville but his mother would never forgive him. Talk about being between the devil and the deep blue sea – only in his case it was Cecily, the Atlantic Ocean and Roger Clements.

'You couldn't resist, could you?'

He jerked his head up at the sound of his mother's sharp voice. Her expression was a mixture of amusement and annoyance. 'Sorry.'

'More problems?'

'Yeah.' There was no point in pretending. They'd always been honest with each other. It'd been only the two of them all his life and Matt didn't miss the father he'd never known. When she considered him old enough his mother told him all about Thomas Robertson without holding anything back or making Matt feel the whole mess was his fault. The brief passion his parents shared hadn't lasted beyond her positive pregnancy test but they'd still been dragooned into marriage by his family. Traditional old Nashville families didn't care for scandal and Thomas was descended from one of the first settlers to the area back in the late 1700s. Dabbling with Cecily, a penniless schoolteacher, was bad enough but driving drunk while running off with a gullible local waitress and crashing into a wall at high speed quite another. The Robertsons paid Cecily off, she reverted to her maiden name and Matt never had anything to do with his father's side of the family. 'I'll sort it later. Promise. I'm not goin' to spoil today.'

'If you need to work this evening I'll understand.'

'I know but that's not happening.' Thanks to the time difference he could stay up late to contact Clint. If it cut into his sleep he'd catch up on the early morning drive over the Alps to Italy, country number five on their speed tour. Over Cecily's shoulder he spotted Betty getting on the bus and heading towards them, frowning.

'Do you know where Sarah is?'

Matt explained he hadn't seen her since they arrived in Rothenburg and listened as she told them about their visit to the Christmas shop. Betty's face coloured up and she stumbled over her words. He didn't need the details of whatever disagreement they'd obviously had. 'I'll go to look for her if you like.' Even this early in the year there were hordes of tourists filling the town and if she didn't want to be found it would be a challenge. Matt slipped his leather jacket back on and stopped on his way off the coach to speak to Kayley. 'If we're not back in time go ahead and leave. Don't worry. I'll find a way for us to catch up with you later.'

Matt hurried across the square and down one of the narrow lanes to the Christmas shop and tried to follow Sarah's thought process. She'd want to blend in so he took a guess she'd choose the busiest street nearby. He took a chance and headed for the one he'd heard was the most popular. The crowds were heavier now that lunch was over but out of the corner of his eye a flash of bright pink caught Matt's attention and he took off running.

'What the heck are you up to?' He seized Sarah's arm, jerking her to a halt before she could step inside a shop. 'Your mom's worried sick about you.'

'Good. So she should be.'

Even Matt was smart enough to recognise a woman who'd been crying. 'How about a cup of tea?' He'd watched enough BBC programmes with his mother to know it was the Brits' go-to consoler for anything from murder to a bad haircut.

'What about the coach?' Sarah hesitated. 'I don't think I can …'

'No problem.' He tucked her arm through his. 'I've instructed the lovely Kayley to go ahead. We'll meet them later when you're ready.'

'You might have a long wait,' she snapped.

'Doesn't matter. Tea first before I take Sleeping Beauty to see her castle.'

'But …'

He touched his finger to her mouth. 'Don't argue. You can't be this close and not indulge your fantasy.' Sarah's mouth settled into a mutinous straight line but she managed a brief nod. It was the best he was likely to get and Matt wasn't stupid enough to press his luck.

Chapter Eleven

Sarah wanted to hold onto her anger but Matt made it hard. He'd been forced on a rescue mission to find her and was stuck with getting them to Innsbruck tonight but didn't appear to be bothered. Leaning back in the chair with one long leg propped comfortably over the other knee he stuck his fork into a large slice of chocolate torte and put a huge bite in his mouth. He'd draped his leather jacket on the back of the chair and she couldn't help noticing the way his dark blue T-shirt brought out the intense colour of his eyes.

'Your mom didn't say what was wrong between the pair of you and you don't have to either. It's your choice.'

Before she could have second thoughts Sarah dumped the whole story on him needing reassurance that she wasn't being unreasonable. 'Go on. Tell me I'm being a complete cow,' she challenged while dreading that he might actually agree.

'Nope. Not gonna do that.' His handsome face creased into a teasing smile. 'Maybe a young calf but not a cow.'

Against her will Sarah had to laugh. 'Was I right to get mad?'

'I think it's understandable and most people would've reacted the same way.' He stabbed another forkful of cake.

'But?'

'But you need to talk to your mom and find out the whole story. There has to be more to it. She loves you and you've told me how she's always had your back.'

Knowing he was right didn't make it any easier to accept.

'How about we do our own thing until tonight and you can collar her before dinner for a chat. Ask for the truth but be careful to listen to her answer.' Matt rested his elbows on the table. 'After you sort things out one way or the other you'll have Kayley's medieval themed extravaganza to take your mind off everything but laughing at me wearing tights.'

'You've got the legs for it. What are you worried about?' she said with a giggle, openly checking him out. 'You could give a young Henry the Eighth a run for his money.'

'Just what I had in mind.' Matt quipped.

'Right. Castle time.' He pushed away the remains of his cake.

'How're we getting there?'

Matt's eyes gleamed. 'Chauffeur driven car. It's the modern day Prince Charming's version of the glass coach.'

Sarah didn't tell him he was getting his fairytales mixed up. 'I'm impressed. How on earth did you have time to get that organised?'

'The wonders of modern technology,' he explained with a grin and waved his mobile phone around. 'A few texts while you were in the ladies' room and we're all set. Come on.' Matt stood and held out his hand. 'Your carriage awaits.'

She didn't care how inappropriate it might be given the "terms" of their agreement but they left the cafe hand in hand.

They didn't talk much in the car but Matt didn't mind.

Sarah missed most of the beautiful scenery after falling asleep with her head on his shoulder and staying that way for the whole two hours. He took advantage and slipped his arm around her, shifting her to rest more comfortably against his chest. Matt occasionally played with her hair, loosely caught up in a ponytail today and smelling of something floral and soft. Once he dared to brush a kiss on her cheek, half hoping she'd stir.

'Over the next hill you will see Neuschwanstein for the first time, sir.' The driver interrupted Matt's thoughts. 'The young lady might wish to be awake.'

'She sure will. Thanks.' Matt blew gently on Sarah's skin and she wriggled around in his arms. 'Time to wake up, Sleeping Beauty.' Her eyes flew open and Matt's chest tightened as she gazed up at him with unguarded desire. 'Your castle awaits.' Pointing out of the window he struggled to regain control of his volatile emotions.

'Oh, wow.' A huge smile lit up her face. 'I was so afraid I'd be disappointed.'

'Hey, Disney never disappoints.'

She poked his arm. 'Don't make fun of my dreams. When I was five this was the epitome of romance before I knew the meaning of the word. I wore out the video and my dad had to buy me another. Althea and I …' Sarah stumbled over her old friend's name. 'We'd take turns playing Princess Aurora and the other would be the evil fairy Maleficent.' She scrutinised Matt. 'I'm not sure you fit the mould of Prince Philip but sometimes a girl has to improvise.'

'Hey. I bet he didn't have a top of the line Mercedes,' Matt protested.

'Being a fairytale prince he naturally rode in on a white horse and I'm sure when they married he whisked her away in a gold carriage but you don't see that bit.' Sarah turned beet red. 'I know it's all make believe, but …'

He rested his finger on her lips. 'Don't apologise, honey, we've all gotta have our dreams.'

'What are yours?' Sarah immediately apologised. 'I'm sorry. I don't know what came over me. It's none of my business.'

For a second he almost confessed to Sarah that his dreams included her, but Matt's sensible side reasserted itself. 'No problem.' He nodded to their driver. 'We'll drive as close as we can to the castle and take some photos. Shame we don't have time for a tour.' Sarah's smile returned and he was relieved he'd done the right thing even if it wasn't the most honest.

What was up with her? Matt's nearness. The exquisite castle. Her mother's startling revelation. All combined to make her more than a little crazy. She'd startled awake in Matt's strong, warm arms with the scent of leather and him filling her senses. Sarah could've sworn the memory drifting away included the imprint of a kiss.

Before everything went wrong she'd have texted Althea and shared the joy of getting to see the castle which featured so prominently in their childish games. A pang of sadness twisted at her stomach and she bit back tears.

'What's wrong?' Matt's simple question finished her off. 'Aw, honey, it's alright.'

'No, it's not and it can't ever be again,' she

sobbed and buried her face in his chest. 'How could they?'

'Maybe you should ask them.' Matt missed little, immediately picking up on what she was talking about. Sarah poured out what was on her heart. How much she missed her old friend. The debilitating sadness at the failure of her marriage. The betrayal she was afraid she'd never get over.

The car crested the next hill and the spectacular countryside spread out in front of them dominated by the fairytale castle high on a hill silenced Sarah's rant.

'If you don't enjoy this moment it's one more thing they've taken from you,' he observed with a wry smile. 'Don't let them succeed.' Matt's vehemence took her by surprise. The impression she got of this conversation not really being about her anymore intensified. 'Roger Clements could destroy my business but I'm not gonna let him. You've got to stand up for yourself. No one else will do it for you.' An angry, hot flush crept up his neck and he pulled over to the far side of the seat to stare blankly out of the car window. 'Ignore me.'

'Can't do that. You let the genie out of the box.' Her feeble attempt at a joke fell flat.

'We will stop in Hohenschwangau. I find a good place for you to take pictures. Okay?' The driver announced his intention. Private cars couldn't get any closer than this small town to view the castle. Sarah promised herself on her next visit she'd ride in one of the horse-drawn carriages up the hill to Neuschwanstein and take the full tour.

'Here will work fine.' Matt spoke up as they made their way along a road opposite a large meadow in front of the town. 'We need to get on to Innsbruck.'

Sarah didn't argue and got out of the car. She'd disrupted his life enough in more ways than one today. Of course he'd done the same to her in return but she'd keep that to herself. 'Could you take a couple of pictures of us together?' She asked the driver. A fleeting grimace dulled Matt's smile but she didn't make any comment. He was tired of this game and Sarah couldn't blame him. 'We're halfway through. Only five more days.'

'Was that supposed to cheer me up?' His dry response was typical. 'Don't answer. Come over here and pretend I'm the prince of your dreams.'

You are. There's no pretence needed on my part. Sarah waited for him to put his arm around her. She'd take what she could get and make the most of it.

Sleeping Beauty's castle at Neuschwanstein with my own handsome prince!

Chapter Twelve

Matt threw his phone on the bed and swore. Clint refused to accept they had a problem. He insisted the new staff would be fine and hinted Matt was making a fuss about nothing.

'Cool it, dude. He's got it all under control. Roger has contacts in New York and thinks we could hit it big there. I told him to go next week and have a look around.'

From the beginning they'd promised to expand only if they were both in agreement. The South was what they both knew so it made sense to get a solid base there first. But Roger flashing dollar signs in Clint's eyes appeared to have scrambled his partner's brains. By the time Matt returned to Nashville he dreaded to imagine what might've been signed and sealed in the name of TekSpeak. He'd promised – or threatened – Clint with another phone call tomorrow. When his old friend changed the subject and asked about Sarah he'd blown him off.

'Ignore the photos. It's a set-up, remember? Yeah. I know she's cute but Sarah's not my type. No way.' Clint might be dumb where Roger Clements was concerned but he'd sure as hell see through Matt's lie if they'd carried on talking.

The flashy blue and gold tunic, fur-trimmed blue cape and leggings mocked Matt from where they hung on the outside of the wardrobe. When he and Sarah arrived it was the only costume Kayley had that was close to being his size. He'd grabbed it without saying a word and stalked off to find his room. No doubt Kayley would switch to interrogation mode to find out what'd gone wrong with her vision of love's young dream.

Matt spotted the minibar in the corner and five minutes later he'd sunk his first beer. By the time he tugged on the ridiculous costume it wasn't the only thing that was fuzzy around the edges.

'Is the time right now?' Sarah set down her handbag and coat on the arm of the sofa.

'Sit down. Please. I can't think while you're standing there glaring at me.'

She grudgingly unfolded her arms and perched on the edge of the bed next to her mother. Using the trick she often employed on her toddlers when they'd misbehaved she didn't say a word.

'What do you want to know?' Betty's voice quavered.

'Everything.'

'I didn't speak up before the wedding because what could I say? That I didn't think Tim loved you enough? And that I was afraid he wouldn't stop his charming ways. You wouldn't have listened.' Her mother sighed. 'I hoped he'd prove me wrong.'

'And Althea?'

'You always looked up to her for reasons I could never understand. I wanted to shake you when you'd sigh and say she was so much prettier and smarter than you.'

'But you didn't?'

Betty dredged up a faint smile. 'Would you have taken any notice? You know from teaching that if you warn one of your little ones off something it makes them want it even more.'

'I suppose you're right.'

They'd negotiated the easiest part, but now came the bit Sarah didn't know if she could get past. 'I told you things weren't good with Tim. You knew we'd been arguing a lot and were struggling to hold our marriage together, at least I was. When did you ...' She clutched her head in her hands and broke down sobbing.

'Oh, my love.' Her mother wrapped her in a warm hug. 'I didn't know anything for sure. I swear I didn't.' Betty whispered. 'People were making remarks about the amount of time Tim spent hanging around the cafe chatting to Althea. I didn't take any notice until I happened to be in there one day and ... saw them.'

'Were they, you know ...' Sarah couldn't spell it out.

'Goodness no. Nothing like that.'

Something inside Sarah shrivelled as her mother explained they'd simply been talking and laughing but it'd been how happy they both looked that struck her. 'Tim wasn't happy with me. When he wasn't working long hours I got the impression he'd rather be anywhere else than with me.' She choked out the words.

'You weren't happy either.'

'No. Near the end we were only really going through the motions of living together,' she whispered. 'But he still shouldn't have ... neither one of them should.'

'Of course they shouldn't. It was selfish and thoughtless.' Her mother's expression hardened. 'But that's the way they both are.'

The gripping pain in her stomach eased and Sarah managed a weak smile. 'You're right.' The rest of the story haltingly emerged and made complete sense. Tim's solitary evening walks had been nothing but a cover for meeting Althea. They'd got careless and were spotted holding hands and kissing along one of the remote country lanes. Gossip soon spread around the village and when it reached her mother's ears she'd been on the verge of telling Sarah when Tim came out and asked for a divorce.

'I kept quiet because I thought I'd only make things worse for you.' Betty's face flushed. 'I was wrong.'

Her mother's quiet admission touched her and she couldn't stay mad any longer. 'Yes, you were, but you did it out of love.' Sarah kissed her mum's cheek. 'If you'd told me I could've challenged him and got out of our marriage with some dignity still intact. Instead I pleaded with him to give us another chance because I couldn't admit we'd never been right for each other in the first place. He wasn't ready to be married to anyone. I only hope he's different this time around for Althea's sake.'

'Are we alright now?' Betty asked.

'Of course. Let's change and have a fun evening. I can't wait to see Matt in costume. He's going to hate it.'

Her mother gave her a searching look but didn't say anymore. No doubt she wouldn't show as much restraint after a couple of glasses of wine.

Matt leaned on the bar, knocked back another beer, and scanned the room. *Oh, yeah*. Sarah's rich burgundy satin dress clung to a figure he'd previously only fantasised about and the low, square neckline showed off her pale, creamy skin. With a circle of pearls woven through her flowing brunette hair she glowed. They might've parted on iffy terms earlier but he'd reverse that right now. Tossing his cape back over one shoulder he strode across the room and planted himself in front of her.

'You're looking mighty pretty tonight, Ms Agnoli.'

Her eyes flared in surprise.

'May I have this dance?' He swept a low bow but almost lost his footing.

'Are you drunk?'

'Only on you, Sarah, only on you.'

'Sitting down might be a better idea.' She grabbed a firm hold of his arm and steered him towards the chairs lined up around the room. 'Have you eaten? Has your mother seen you?'

The questions made his head spin. To stop her talking Matt seized Sarah by the shoulders and planted a hard kiss on her glossy, dark red lips.

'Behave.' Sarah shoved him away. 'Sit.' Her sharp tone cut through the fog in his brain and he slumped in the nearest chair. 'I'm going to fetch us some food. Don't you dare move until I get back.'

Matt attempted a sloppy salute but gave up.

'Start eating.' She thrust a plate of food at him.

The sight of the glistening slices of rare roast beef and pile of potatoes turned his stomach but under Sarah's fierce glare he began to eat. Halfway through she made him stop and drink a large glass of water. Matt ate as much as he could manage before setting the plate down on the floor. 'Happy now?'

'Drink more water.' Another glass was forced on him and he gulped it down. 'Feeling any better?'

'I guess.' He'd never been much of a drinker and combined with not eating since half a slice of cake at lunchtime it'd gone straight to his head.

'Uh, oh, your mother's headed this way. Leave this to me,' she hissed. 'Cecily.' Sarah jumped up. 'Aren't you looking wonderful. What a beautiful dress. Happy Birthday.'

'Thank you, sweetie.'

'Poor Matt turned his ankle coming down the stairs. He feels awful that he won't be able to dance with you.'

I do?

'I'm sure.' His mother's sarcasm laced response cut through him. She obviously thought he'd talked Sarah into lying for him to get out of displaying his non-existent dancing skills in public.

Matt pushed himself up to standing. 'It's not too bad. I'm sure I can manage one dance.' Behind his mother's back Sarah shook her head violently but he ignored her. 'May I?' He held out his hand and led her into the centre of the room. The music started up again but instead of a slow number like they'd been playing before the band launched into a lively song. Matt managed a couple of leaping steps but when he tried to twirl his mother around his left shoe suddenly flew off. He tripped and landed on his back on the floor with a hard thump.

'Grab my hand,' his mother ordered but his strength seeped away and he simply lay there. 'You're drunk,' she declared, bending down to sniff his breath. Matt was too tired to argue. The last thing he remembered before everything went black was the sympathy written all over Sarah's face as she stood over him. *She cares for you. Worth getting drunk.*

Chapter Thirteen

Matt closed his eyes against the blazing sunshine pouring in through the coach windows. He'd been the last to arrive and all fifty-eight passengers stared openly at him with varying expressions on their faces ranging from amused to disgusted.

'You've got four hours to catch up with your sleep. You'll miss the most stunning scenery of the whole trip but it's your own fault.'

Ouch. He wouldn't easily be forgiven for messing up his mother's birthday party. Matt thought he remembered her helping him into bed but wasn't going to ask for confirmation. There'd been no time for checking emails before he left this morning and Kayley had warned them yesterday that the internet connections in Venice would be the worst of the whole trip. Roger Clements would be pleased.

'I'm going to sit with Betty. I'd prefer to be able to talk with someone who'll do more than grunt in return,' Cecily announced and he didn't protest.

'Water and aspirins.'

Matt opened one eye. He wasn't too hung over to appreciate the cheerful yellow blouse and white jeans enhancing Sarah's fresh, simple beauty this morning so perhaps he might be on track to survive. 'Thanks.' He took the couple of pills she held out and washed them down with half a bottle of water.

'Your mum's, um, not happy is she?'

'I believe pissed is the word.' He winced. 'Might as well say it like it is. I don't blame her either. I'm a moron.'

'I was almost mean enough to take your picture last night but I resisted the temptation.' Sarah's eyes danced with amusement. 'Before you drift off to sleep I want to thank you.'

He couldn't imagine what he'd done recently to warrant anything apart from scorn.

'My mum and I are good now because of you making me listen to her.'

'That's great.' Matt thought he should probably ask for more details but his throbbing head couldn't cope. 'Tell me more later.'

She smirked, gesturing towards the front of the coach. 'Kayley's about to start today's running commentary so it'll be much later. Good luck trying to sleep.'

'Listen up everyone. We're coming up on the Europabrücke, or Europe bridge and it's spectacular so don't miss checking it out as we go across. At one time it was Europe's highest bridge and it's the main route across the Alps from western Austria to the South Tyrol in Italy. Look out for bungee jumpers because it's a popular spot. Anyone fancy having a go?'

'Maybe she'll try it with a defective cord,' Matt whispered in Sarah's ear, setting her off in a fit of giggles she gamely tried to suppress. 'See you in Venice.' He winked and leaned back against the window before closing his eyes.

She hadn't had the heart to insist on the window seat so Sarah spent the next few hours leaning over Matt's comatose body to make the most of the wonderful scenery. Alpine valleys reminding her of *The Sound of Music*, picturesque castles and the soaring Dolomite

Mountains all imprinted themselves on her memory. Tiring of listening to Kayley's grating voice she briefly leaned against Matt's shoulder and closed her eyes. His broad shoulders were a perfect resting spot.

'My picture of you with your mouth gaping open is trending on Facebook.'

Sarah jerked awake and met Matt's laughing eyes, as bright a shade of blue as today's sunny sky. 'You'd better be joking.'

He flung up his hands. 'No phone signal. Promise.'

'Where are we?'

'On the outskirts of Venice.'

Sarah's heart raced. With everything that'd been going on she'd come close to forgetting one of the main reasons they'd chosen this particular trip in the first place. Oddly enough her mother hadn't wanted to discuss contacting her dad's relatives since they left home.

'Do your father's family know you're coming?'

'No. To be honest I'm not certain they know we exist.' She admitted. 'Dad often talked vaguely about getting back in touch but I don't know if he actually did. One Christmas when he was in a reflective mood he implied they might not want to hear from him.'

'Why?'

She shrugged. He'd refused to say and never spoke of it again. Then it was too late. 'Mum won't talk about it either although I suspect that's more because she'd ashamed of how little she knows. I don't think she ever pressed my father very much. Originally she was all in favour of contacting them when we knew we'd be here but now she seems to have changed her mind.'

'Pay attention, speed daters.' Kayley clapped her hands. 'We'll be parking soon. Our driver will unload and we'll get a water taxi to our hotel. If you've got the small bags I recommended for tonight well done. If not you'll be hauling everything yourselves and there's quite a lot of walking. I did warn you.'

'Yes, ma'am,' Matt gently mocked and the touch of playfulness made Sarah fall a little harder for him, as it did every time. She suspected that was because it was out of kilter with his personality. 'If you've got a phone number for the Agnolis I could call for you from the hotel. My Italian's good enough they should understand me.'

Trusting him was a big step and Sarah hesitated.

'I'm not gonna throw a fit if you say no.' His engaging grin made her heart flutter. 'I'll still let you photograph me in embarrassing situations.'

His casual reminder of everything he'd done for her hit home. She was being stupid. Sarah needed to do this for her own sake even if her mother had chickened out and Matt's language skills might be the key to helping her succeed. 'Thanks. I'll take you up on the offer.' She startled when he suddenly clasped her right hand and raised it to his lips, brushing a soft kiss over her fingers.

'You are a very lovely woman, Ms Agnoli. I wish you weren't.'

Before she could ask for an explanation Matt abruptly let go of her hand and busied himself slipping on his leather jacket and zipping up his backpack. Maybe it was better not to know what'd brought that on.

You idiot. Matt hadn't learned when to keep his mouth

shut. Ever since he'd met Sarah everything was out of whack and he wasn't sure how to get back on track. *Do you even want to?* His distraction was seeping over to his work. The old Matt would've pinned Roger Clements to the wall long before now but, although he'd made a lot of noise, he hadn't actually *done* anything. He was using his mother as an excuse but that's all it was. On their last night in Paris he'd take Sarah on a proper date and hopefully get it out of his system. Losing a twenty dollar bet would be worth it to get back his sanity.

'Come on, Dopey.' Sarah poked his arm.

Matt trailed off the coach after her and every minute of the next hour reminded him why he hadn't wanted to come on this trip in the first place. Much as Kayley annoyed him the woman deserved a gold medal. She herded everyone through the narrow streets, onto a water taxi, off the other end and along to their destination. Somehow they ended up at the hotel with the right number of people and suitcases without anyone falling into the murky canals.

He pulled Sarah to one side as Kayley was handing out keys. 'Come to my room when you've dropped off your bags.'

'Very direct aren't you? Most women prefer a more subtle approach.' He caught the tremor underneath her laughter and guessed she was using humour as a cover for extreme nerves.

Matt swung his heavy, old-fashioned brass key in her face. 'Even you shouldn't be able to mess this one up. I'll see you soon.'

In his tiny room he stripped off and levered himself into the tiny shower for the fastest wash on record. He threw on a clean shirt with his same black jeans and raked a comb through his unruly hair. Matt almost missed the soft tap on the door.

'Welcome to my spacious abode.' Over Sarah's shoulder he caught sight of his mother staring at him from across the hall with a mixture of disbelief and satisfaction.

Chapter Fourteen

Sarah squealed as Matt yanked her into the room and slammed the door.

'Sorry. My mother saw us.'

'And you panicked. Despite the fact our purpose for meeting is completely innocent.' *Apart from the fact your hair is damp and curling in a really appealing way and I can smell the fresh lime soap you've just used and I really, really want to …* Sarah stamped on her treacherous libido and forced herself to remember why she was in Matt's room. She held out the piece of paper she'd sneaked out of her mother's handbag.

'If they're interested in meeting do you want to skip sightseeing and go straight on over?'

'Yes.' Sarah rushed to agree before she could change her mind. 'If my mum wants to come she can.'

Matt nodded and brought out his phone. There were several minutes of incomprehensible Italian conversation, at least it was to her, until he said *ciao* – the only word she recognised. 'All set. I said we'll be there by three.'

'We?'

He raised one eyebrow skywards. 'How're you goin' to talk to each other if I don't go? Their English isn't great and I'm pretty sure your Italian begins and ends with *ciao*.' The quirk of laughter pulling at his mouth irked her. Why did he have to be right quite as often? 'It's alright, honey, I don't expect an apology. Go and talk to your mother while I get transport lined up. I'm guessin' we'll need to leave here around two.'

'Fine.' Sarah's short response made him smile. 'Thanks.'

'There, that didn't kill you did it?'

She tossed her head in the air and left the room with his laughter ringing in her ears. Sarah climbed the stairs to the next floor and used her oversized key to open the door, unable to stop smiling as she remembered her first meeting with Matt. Her mother was staring out of the window.

'How's the room? Is everything alright. By the way I've rung the Agnolis. Well, Matt did it for me actually.' She rattled off the plans they'd made. 'Do you want to come?' Her mother shook her head and a heavy silence hung in the air. 'Why not?'

'Because there are things concerning his family that your father never spoke of. If he didn't want me to know I think it's best if I leave it alone. I'm going to join Cecily on the gondola ride and visit to the Murrano glassworks.'

Sarah didn't push. 'I'll tell you how I get on when we return.'

'I'm sure you will.'

'Right, I'm off to meet Matt downstairs. I'll see you later.' Sarah checked her handbag for her purse and camera.

'I'm glad he's going with you.'

She almost cracked a joke about Betty and Cecily's continuing attempts at matchmaking but the worry etched into her mother's face stopped her. 'Me too.'

Matt didn't bother to argue with his mother when she collared him in his room and dropped very unsubtle hints about how well he was getting on with Sarah.

Let her think what she liked. Gathering up his things, he gave his laptop a longing glance before hiding it in one of the drawers. They'd walk and get a water taxi back to the parked coach where a regular taxi should be waiting to drive them outside of the city to the village of Monticaruso. He hadn't been entirely truthful with Sarah. The Agnoli family hadn't been at all keen for her to visit and it'd taken all of Matt's diplomatic skills to talk Senor Agnoli around. Agnoli had muttered something about people who foolishly thought they could make things right. Matt's other lie came in the form of playing down the Italian man's competent grasp of English to give him an excuse to accompany Sarah.

Downstairs he found her waiting in the lobby, alone. 'No Betty?'

'She refused to come.' Sarah half-smiled. 'She's going sightseeing with your mother so goodness knows what they'll get up to.'

Matt played along and suggested a few crazy things to make her laugh. 'Come on. Let's go on our detective expedition.' He took hold of her arm and tucked it through his. 'For safety. To protect you from the local Romeos.'

'Shouldn't you save that for tomorrow when we go to Verona? You know we'll have to recreate the famous balcony scene for Facebook don't you?' Her eyes shone and he wished he could keep her smiling at him forever. *Forever? Where did that come from?*

They walked together and despite his longer legs Matt found she kept up with him easily. When he'd been in Venice once before on business he'd found the city to be dirty and run down, literally crumbling away into the canals, but through Sarah's eyes it came to life. She told him stories of the Renaissance princes, the fantastic masked balls and the intrigues that'd gone on in every corner of the city. They stopped on the Rialto Bridge for a photo and Matt read the caption Sarah posted.

Romance Italian style! Venetian men have nothing on my Nashville dreamboat — or should that be gondola. LOL.

Matt wondered when he'd started to wish she meant all these things.

By some miracle their taxi was on time and Sarah's chatter stopped as they drove away from the city.

'Hey, I could do with your input. Tell me what you think about this.' Matt tried to take her mind off where they were headed and help himself at the same time. She didn't interrupt once as he poured out his growing problems with TekSpeak.

'I'm no businesswoman but children are only tiny people and Roger Clements is the same as a toddler trying to prove himself to the bigger boys. He wants to run and play with them before he's ready and doesn't like to be told no.'

That all made sense but Matt didn't see how it helped.

'You need to give him firm directions and limits while dangling a carrot in front of his nose. Promise Roger that if he follows your instructions now he'll be rewarded in the long term. You need to get Clint on your side as well in the same way both parents need to be on board in disciplining a child.'

'You're a genius.' Matt popped a quick kiss on her forehead. She didn't object when he took hold of her hand but he'd opened himself up to a subtle form of torture because she leaned her head on his shoulder. The warmth of her body pressed against him and the aroma of her clean citrus perfume made him painfully aware of his growing desire for her.

As they turned off the main autostrada and drove through the countryside Matt couldn't help admiring the people who grew grapes and olives on hilly, terraced land that should've been impossible to farm.

'Casa Agnoli is up here.' The driver turned onto a hilly track leading off to the right and they bounced along the rocky narrow road. Matt suspected the shocks on the car were long since gone. Out of the blue the road widened and led them to a set of black wrought iron gates fronting an elegant white-painted villa with the typical red-tiled roof and requisite wooden shutters on every window. Matt let out a long, low whistle as the gates opened automatically and they drove in. The large, colourful garden, collection of expensive cars parked out front and swimming pool off to one side indicated this was no run-of-the-mill farmhouse.

'Goodness.'

'Not what you expected?'

Sarah shook her head. 'I always got the impression my grandparents were poor and that my father left Italy for a better life. I suppose we'd better do this now we're here.' She jumped from the car and headed towards the front door. Matt scrambled out after her and gave the driver instructions to wait before he hurried to catch up.

A short, stocky man appeared at the door and his fierce, dark eyes bored into them. 'So you're here. I suppose you had better come in.'

Sarah didn't move. 'And you are?'

'*Zio* Luigi. Your uncle. Roberto was my older brother.'

'Brother?' She stumbled over her words. 'He never mentioned having a brother.'

'Not surprising,' Luigi grunted and headed back into the house.

'I guess he expects us to follow him.'

They walked up the steps together and entered the cool, marble-tiled hall. For the second time in as many minutes Matt couldn't hide his surprise. He squeezed Sarah's hand as she threw him a look of utter panic.

Chapter Fifteen

Sarah stared around at the mass of people congregating in the large hall, all talking loudly and gesticulating in her direction. In the midst of the chaos she couldn't help noticing the elegant spiral staircase disappearing behind them all to an upper floor and the impressive collection of paintings around the walls. An older man, eerily resembling her father, stepped forward and held out his hands.

'Welcome to Casa Agnoli. I am your *nonno*, your grandfather Enzo.'

A stunning brunette squeezed into a skin-tight red dress launched into a string of Italian and by her tone and accompanying gestures they weren't words of welcome. Her grandfather remonstrated with the fireball but she wouldn't shut up and kept pointing her sharp fingernails in Sarah's direction.

'What's wrong? Who is she?' No one answered immediately until her grandfather finally murmured something. 'Matt. Tell me what he said.'

Matt's deep blue eyes shone with compassion. 'Her name is Francesca and it appears she is your half-sister.'

Sarah swayed on her feet and only Matt's firm hand around her waist kept her upright. 'That's a lie,' she half-whispered. 'How can she be? My father would never …'

'I don't know, honey. Hopefully we can find out.'

'My *nonno* he is not a liar,' Francesca scoffed.

'Come in. We will have wine and sweets before we

talk,' her grandfather said and led the way out of the hall.

'I'm sorry to have dragged you into all of this.' She squeezed Matt's hand and got a warm smile in return.

'I'm glad you didn't come alone. Let's go.'

'Sarah. Sit by me.' Senor Agnoli beckoned her across the room and she let go of Matt's hand. The massive rectangular room with its soaring extravagantly decorated ceiling, opulent furniture and crystal chandeliers only made her more unsettled and she hurried to join her grandfather. '*Per favore*, Maria.' A stooped elderly woman swathed in black slowly carried around a silver tray with glasses of wine. Sarah listened impatiently as Enzo went into every proud detail about the Chianti they were drinking, a product of the Agnoli family's vineyards. She dutifully drank hers and forced down one of Maria's supposedly famous almond cookies. All the time she was acutely aware of everyone staring and talking about her – some things it wasn't necessary to speak the language to understand.

'Your mother is well? I hoped she would come with you.' Enzo frowned.

Sarah hurried to explain about the holiday they were on. 'It's called a European Speed Date and today is our only chance to explore Venice. She didn't want to miss it.' The lame excuse was the best she could come up with to explain her mother's absence and she suspected her grandfather guessed the truth. She set her empty glass down on the marble-topped table. Sarah longed to plunge right in and ask about her supposed half-sister but bided her time. 'I would like to know more about my father and his life here. He

86

rarely mentioned his family and my mother says there were things he would never talk about to her. She was content to let things be but I'm not,' she said.

Her grandfather's lined face creased into an indulgent smile. 'Your father was always a spirited boy. You take after him.'

'That is simply another way of saying he was disobedient and reckless.' Luigi butted in, 'Some of us were left to pick up the pieces.'

Francesca leapt from her chair and let forth another torrent of fierce Italian. Sarah's uncle shouted back, gesticulating wildly.

'*Silenzio*,' Enzo shouted and they went quiet. '*Scusa*, Sarah, they forget themselves. You are our guest and should be treated with respect.'

'Thank you, but I still need to know the truth.'

'So be it.' Her grandfather shrugged and began to speak. Sarah shifted on the sofa to make room for Matt who'd quietly come across to join her.

'As my oldest son, Roberto was expected to take over the family vineyard and estate, marry a local girl and continue the Agnoli legacy.' Enzo's eyes clouded over with pain. 'Francesca's mother is called Serafina and she, Roberto and Luigi were all childhood friends. Her family live over the next hill and our families have always been close,' Enzo explained. 'Serafina was a beauty, like my dear Francesca and you know how young people are. Teenagers do not always stop to think of the consequences of their actions. One day Serafina's father, Gino, came to see me and he was very angry. He insisted that Roberto must marry Serafina because she was to have his baby.' Enzo's features hardened. 'Your father refused. He insisted that he cared for her very much but they did not love each other. I told him that did not matter but he closed his heart to me and said he would leave to stay with a friend in London.' Enzo rested his hands on his knees, breathing heavily. 'Roberto promised to work and send money to Serafina but Gino wanted nothing from him. Gino came up with the idea of Luigi marrying her instead. He insisted no one ever needed to know he was not the baby's father.'

'I can't believe my father ...' Sarah's breath caught in a sob.

'Roberto was not a bad boy,' Enzo muttered, 'I see now that he was young and scared but at the time I could not forgive him. He did try to reconcile with us later but I rejected him for good after he announced he had married an English girl and had a daughter.'

'Francesca is *my* daughter in every way that is important and I hope Serafina will say I have been a good husband.' Luigi's face reddened.

'Do you have any other children?' Sarah ventured.

'It was not to be.' He gazed fondly at his daughter. 'She is more precious for that. Even if Francesca could do with learning some manners.' Luigi's indulgent smile made it clear he would always forgive her.

'I would like to meet your mother,' Luigi announced with a grim smile. 'I missed my brother every single day and I regret never seeing him again. I need to hear her talk of him.'

Sarah threw Matt a pleading glance.

'Maybe it would be better if Sarah explains all of this to Betty first. It will be a tremendous shock and she may need time to think about it before deciding if she would like to meet you all.'

'You are a good man,' Enzo said. 'My granddaughter is a lucky woman. When are you going to make an honest woman of her? We will all come and dance at your wedding.'

Sarah nearly choked and didn't know where to look.

Matt floundered and Sarah only gazed blankly at him. 'Um, we are very good friends but we only met last week.'

'Time is nothing where the heart is concerned.' Her grandfather cracked a broad smile. 'I met my beloved Maddelena on *Domenica delle Palme*, Palm Sunday, and by the feast of *San Marco*, the patron saint of *Venezia*, four weeks later she was my wife. We were blessed to have forty-seven wonderful years together.'

'That's wonderful. I think it's time we left now,' Sarah finally spoke. 'Our taxi is waiting and my mother will worry if we're late.' Matt stood up before they could be drawn into any more questions about his intentions – good, bad or otherwise.

'Of course.'

Everyone started to talk at once and tried to introduce themselves to Sarah and Matt before they left. His head spun with attempting to translate when necessary and trying to sort out the various cousins from hordes of nieces and nephews.

Finally they managed to get away and sat together in the back seat of the taxi, loaded down with bottles of Agnoli wine, local olive oil and huge branches of almond blossom cut from the trees outside the villa.

'Kayley will have a fit when she sees this lot,' Matt joked as they waved to everyone out of the back window. 'Are you okay?' He touched Sarah's shoulder. 'Your father loved you very much. Nothing you've heard today changes that.'

Her huge brown eyes brimmed over with tears. 'I know, but it's still hard. I worshipped him and now I wonder …'

'Don't,' Matt said. 'He was a good father and Francesca has a good father too in Luigi. You don't know how lucky you are.'

'Will you tell me about your father one day?'

Her question surprised him although he supposed it shouldn't have. 'I guess so. If you want.'

'I do. My *nonno* was right. You are a good man.' She brushed a kiss against his cheek.

The touch of her soft lips, the fragrance of almond flowers filling the air, and Sarah's heartfelt words pushed him to be reckless. Matt cradled her face with his hands and drew her to him.

'Kiss me.'

Her breathy plea released the passion he'd stamped on too long and in a blinding flash of intuition Matt knew Enzo was right. Matt forced himself to let go of Sarah before he completely forgot where they were. 'Later,' his voice rasped.

'Yes.' She leaned closer so their foreheads touched. 'First I've got to talk to my mother.'

'Come and see me when you're done. I'm good at mopping up tears.'

'You're good at a lot of things.' She glanced up at him from under her long, dark lashes and a nugget of coldness buried deep inside him melted away.

'But for now …' Matt stopped the conversation with another sizzling kiss.

Chapter Sixteen

The sight of her mother's face when she told her about Serafina and Francesca would haunt her forever.

'You warned me not to go, but ...'

Her mother struggled to smile. 'You've never listened to me before so I don't know why I thought you'd start now.'

'How was your day?'

'My day?' Betty's eyebrows rose skywards. 'You tell me my precious husband had a child with another woman before we were married and you ask how my sightseeing trip went? I've been thinking about you all afternoon.'

In the taxi she'd gone back and forth in her head as to whether she regretted going to Casa Agnoli and come to the conclusion she'd made the right decision. Matt's quiet presence had given her the space to think, making her love him more. *Love him?* Where did that come from?

'I'm really sorry, Mum.'

'I know you are. It's done now.'

That was the closest she'd get to being forgiven. 'How do you feel about going out to dinner with Matt and his mother if they don't have any other plans?'

'I suppose we could.' Her mother kicked off her shoes. 'I'm going to take a nap first. You can organise things and wake me up when it's time to get ready.'

This time Sarah made sure to check the corridor before tapping on Matt's door. He opened it in the middle of buttoning up a clean blue shirt and Sarah couldn't help staring. Clearly sitting in front of a computer screen wasn't all he did because there were well-defined muscles facing her that no one acquired unless they worked out regularly.

'How did it go?'

Somehow she stumbled over the dinner suggestion.

'Sure. That'll be great.' He pulled her to him, stroking his large, warm hands down to rest around her waist. 'Will they mind eating late?' Matt lowered his mouth to hers and Sarah was lost.

Matt watched her sleep and wished he could stop time. If they didn't move soon the danger of discovery-by-mothers grew stronger. He groaned as Sarah wriggled back against him and couldn't resist snaking his arms around her and snuggling closer to press soft, feathery kisses on her neck.

'Love me again,' she whispered.

He ought to be sensible and logical but he wouldn't because she'd bewitched him as surely as if she'd cast a spell over them both. Instead he did exactly as she'd asked, arousing her quickly and making her his again. There'd be the chance for lingering and slow another day. *Will there?*

'Don't,' Sarah murmured, burying her head in his chest.

'Don't what?' He needed her to spell it out to be sure he wasn't getting this all wrong. He didn't get the impression that Sarah was the sort of girl jump into bed with any man, but they were on holiday away from their normal lives and she'd received a serious shock today.

'You're over thinking again, aren't you?'

Matt propped himself on one elbow. He couldn't make a rational reply while he was close enough to smell his own scent lingering on Sarah's creamy skin. 'I care for you very much.'

'But?'

There were so many "buts" he didn't know which to choose first. 'Where do you see this going?' He'd throw the ball in her court and see where she tossed it.

Sarah sat up too and covered herself with the sheet. 'I wasn't expecting you to drop on one knee under Juliet's balcony tomorrow but this meant something to me and …' She blinked back tears. 'I took it for granted it did to you too. Was I wrong?' When he hesitated a shade too long she threw back the covers, jumped out of bed and quickly started to tug on her clothes.

'Of course it did.' Matt hurried to reassure her but didn't succeed by the hurt etched into her face.

'Can you bear to keep our dinner arrangement?' Sarah hurried on before he could explain himself. 'Things are a bit tricky with my mum so you'd be helping me out. Also we haven't done any photos today.'

The harsh words put him back in his place but Matt couldn't complain. 'Of course.' He got out of bed and kept his back to her while he pulled on his abandoned boxer shorts. What he ached to say was how beautiful she looked, flushed and tousled from their lovemaking, and that it'd been special for him too. But he didn't because as usual he couldn't find the right words. 'Sarah, don't be mad with me, please. I understand computers, but I'm not good with relationships. I always get it wrong.' A brief flash of sympathy flitted across her face but she didn't say another word only gave a slight shrug and turned away. Then she walked out of the door leaving Matt to stare blankly at the space where she'd been.

All she wanted was to crawl into bed, pull up the covers and wake up back home in Cornwall. She'd ruined her mother's holiday with her insistence on dragging out long buried family secrets and made a fool of herself over another man. In the village pantomime she specialised in painting scenery and organising the props but she'd hung around enough rehearsals and performances to pick up a few acting basics. For the next four days she'd have to put that knowledge to good use. Nobody must have a clue to the pain gnawing at her deep inside. She'd been exposed to enough ridicule after her marriage failed and refused to open herself up again to everyone's sympathy.

While her mother napped Sarah took a long, hot shower and found the new red dress she'd bought on a whim one Christmas but never worn. Slipping it on she checked her appearance in the mirror. The silky material flattered her figure but the plunging neckline and generous side-slit were far more daring than she remembered. Matt's reticent reply to her question hammered into her and she froze in the middle of zipping up the dress. She'd show him. Sarah carefully applied her make-up before adding a slick of glossy red lipstick and a spritz of her favourite perfume for good measure.

Sarah put a bright smile on her face and woke her mother up. 'Matt suggested we try a restaurant on St. Mark's Square that's supposed to be wonderful. We're meeting them downstairs at eight.'

'You're looking, um, quite fancy tonight. I'd better

smarten myself up if I'm going to rival *that* dress.'
Betty smiled. 'Of course there's no handsome man to
notice what I'm wearing so it's different for you.'

Sarah blushed and glanced away, hoping her
mother would take her reticence as embarrassment.
She went out on the miniscule balcony and wrote a
few postcards to avoid any more questions.

'I'm ready when you are.' Her mother stuck her
head out around the door. With another forced smile
plastered over her face Sarah prepared to endure a
long, agonizing evening.

Until she sat opposite to Matt across the dinner table
Sarah couldn't have imagined it being this hard. To see
him again, to smell his distinctive cologne and listen
to his deep, soft drawl without being able to touch
him was torture. Instead of wearing tonight's crisp
white shirt and dark grey trousers, Sarah pictured him
naked, stretched out in the bed and reaching for her.
The one time she met his gaze full on a dark flush of
heat coloured his neck.

Italy had turned on a mild, spring evening for them
to enjoy and Sarah wished she could truly savour the
moment. Sparkling white lights glittered around the
square highlighting the magnificent ancient buildings
and the sound of water lapping in the background and
other people's laughter drifting in the air made her
inner emptiness more acute.

'Matt tells me you met some of your father's family
today. That must've been interesting?' Cecily put
Sarah on the spot. She'd no clue how much he'd told
his mother and didn't want to embarrass Betty by
saying too much.

'The countryside is really quite something and Casa Agnoli was spectacular.' Matt's effort to help her out touched Sarah. She relaxed enough to describe the villa and adjoining vineyard without going into details about the family. 'How about we get someone to take a photo of us all?' She wished she could express her appreciation to him for rescuing her again. Matt called the waiter over and passed him the phone before encouraging them all to move closer together. Every nerve in her body tensed when he draped his arm around her shoulder. 'Smile. It's not an execution,' he whispered in her ear.

Then why does it feel like it?

'That should be a good one. Seeing a picture of us with our mothers should get them thinking.'

Sarah wished she could throw the stupid phone in the canal. Tim and Althea didn't care where she was or who she was with, and why should they? In a vague way they'd be pleased to see her happy but that was as far as it would go.

'Brilliant.' She flashed another fake smile. 'I'm going for a walk. I won't be long.' Sarah escaped and hurried across the square. Near a flower seller she stopped and did her Facebook post.

A beautiful night in Venice, one of the most romantic cities on the planet, and I couldn't be happier! We've had a wonderful meal with our mothers who are already great friends. Life is good.

The whole day had been a tangle of deceits and disappointments. Sarah's only consolation was that surely tomorrow couldn't be any worse?

Chapter Seventeen

Matt cursed the crappy internet connection, his own stupidity and his mother's persistence.

What's going on with you and Sarah? Don't tell me you've messed up again. I'll talk to her if it will help. Her mother's such a nice woman and she agrees with me.

Watching Sarah rub in what he was missing by wearing that damn red dress had only irritated him more. None of them understood.

Maybe at least his phone would work. Something had to in this useless place. Yesterday Sarah opened his eyes to the beauties of Venice but today it'd gone back to being a dreary, dirty, crumbling city. Roger's sleepy voice grunted down the line and Matt got a nasty kick of pleasure from knowing he'd woken the other man up.

'Sorry to disturb you.' *Not really but I've been raised to be a well-mannered Southern boy.* 'I want the rundown on Atlanta and everything you found out in New York.' *You're not going to flannel me any longer.* He listened and made notes, preparing to tear Roger's plans to shreds. It was no surprise to hear that the manager he and Clint handpicked was refusing to work with Roger's sub-standard recruits. Roger hadn't kept on top of the contractors because he'd taken time out to go to New York so things were lagging in the office refit and unless a miracle occurred they wouldn't be able to open on time.

'New York could be a challenge,' Roger admitted. 'Costing might be an issue.'

No shit. He let his colleague ramble on and dig himself into a deeper hole with every word he uttered. 'What's Clint saying to all this?' Matt had started to send regular messages to his partner peppered with seemingly innocuous questions. Despite getting few replies he knew his old friend would be taking it all in and making up his own mind.

'He's not too happy.'

Bingo.

'He told me to call you later.' Roger sighed. 'We need you to get in touch with the Atlanta manager and try to placate him.'

'I'll be happy to do that but you need to fire your recruits today and rehire the original people if they'll still work for us. Offer them a bonus and grovel. I don't care what it takes,' Matt spelled it out. 'Have you signed any commitments in New York?'

'Nope. Clint wouldn't let me.'

Thank God. 'I'll call Atlanta this afternoon when it's beginning of the work day there. From now on I want twice daily reports and you're not to agree to anything unless it's approved by myself and Clint. You'll be on a tight leash until you prove yourself.'

'Yes, sir, I'm sorry.'

Matt heard the defeat in Roger's voice. Deep down he wasn't a bad young man but he lacked judgment, something that would hopefully come with experience. 'Learn from this and you'll be okay.'

'You're not going to sack me?'

'Consider yourself on probation. Now go back to bed and get some sleep.' He turned his phone off and shoved it back in his pocket. If he didn't hurry he'd be late for the bus and annoying his mother yet again wouldn't be smart.

Sarah's heart raced as Matt leapt onto the bus and she struggled to ignore how sexy he looked this morning. His dark blond hair caught the light and she remembered his rumbling laughter as she'd run her hands through the thick wavy strands yesterday. He flashed his mother a broad smile and dropped into the seat by her. The irony that this morning's only sightseeing stop was to Verona and Juliet's balcony wasn't lost on Sarah. It would be their only real break before the long drive to Lucerne and Switzerland, the last new country on their list.

'I didn't sleep well. I'm going to try to nap until we get there,' Sarah declared with a yawn. She couldn't think of any other way to avoid her mother's persistent questions. Cecily and Betty had ganged up to pressure their wayward children and weren't going to be easily put off. Sarah closed her eyes and ignored her mother's exaggerated sigh.

'Time for *amore*, speed-daters.' Sarah jerked awake as Kayley clapped her hands. 'You have two hours before I need you back here. The tour of Juliet's house is included in your vacation package and don't miss your photo op on the balcony, ladies! I'll be looking for my own Romeo.' She giggled and Sarah forced down the urge to strangle her. 'Off we go. Chop, chop.'

She trailed off the coach and wondered how she could lose her mother for a while.

'Come on, let's beat the crowd.' Matt's voice next to her ear made her jump. '*Casa di Giulietta* first stop.'

Sarah didn't move. Did he really expect to slip right back into their old, mildly flirtatious friendship after the way he'd treated her yesterday? The man must be as inhuman as his computers.

'Yeah, I know I'm an ass,' he muttered. 'There's a ton of things I want to say but the first one is thank you.'

Whatever for? Great sex? Not cutting off your privates when you made it clear our lovemaking meant nothing more to you than a quick holiday fling?

'Thanks to you I got Clint back on board and we've put Roger in his place. Hopefully we can salvage the Atlanta project without too much loss of face.'

'That's good. I'm glad my idea helped,' she said stiffly.

Matt shuffled from one foot to the other, finally meeting her stare directly for the first time. 'You sure looked beautiful last night. That red dress was something else. I didn't know how to keep from touching you.'

'You appeared to manage admirably.'

'Oh, Sarah.' He let out a heavy sigh. 'I don't do opening up well. It freaks me out.' The simple statement tugged at her heart but she refused to soften. 'Can we have coffee and I promise I'll talk?'

'Be careful. You might be on dangerous ground. Talking has been known to damage people for life.'

'I'll take a chance if you will.' Matt held out his hand and the sight of his trembling fingers persuaded Sarah to give in.

The gleam in her mother's eyes when Sarah hurried over to tell her she was going to hang out with Matt could've illuminated a dark cave.

'Come on. Cement my doom.' He took hold of her hand and they walked across the square to the furthest cafe away from the coach and settled at a table near the back, hopefully well away from prying eyes.

Once the waiter set tiny cups of rich, dark espresso in front of them and left them alone they couldn't avoid each other anymore.

'Time is our enemy, isn't it?' His wry observation made her smile. 'Normal people can take things gradually and get to know each other. We don't have that luxury.'

'Has that method worked well for you before now?' Sarah asked. It certainly hadn't for her. She and Tim were friends for years but when they married it'd still been a miserable failure.

'Not really.' Matt shook his head.

'Give me the potted history of Matthew Anderson. I don't even know if it is Matthew?' She glanced at her watch. 'You've got five minutes.'

'Start the timer.' He grinned and started to count on his fingers. 'Matthew Thomas Anderson. Thirty-eight years of age. Brought up by a single mother in Nashville, Tennessee. Story of my father to come later. You know my work. Hobbies are few but serious, I don't do casual well in anything. Swimming – fifty laps most mornings. Marathon running. Oh and reading the sort of heavy, financial books most people avoid like the plague.'

She blushed remembering the intensity of their lovemaking. Everything this man did would be to the hilt and if he ever fell in love it would be to the same degree. The lucky woman would never have cause to doubt him.

'Your father?' Matt's features darkened and Sarah almost wished the question unasked but couldn't back down now.

'He was a bit of a playboy.' The disdain lacing his voice was at odds with the blank expression he'd put on to cover up his emotions. Sarah listened quietly to his story and couldn't help wishing his mother had perhaps been more reticent. Over-sharing wasn't always a good thing where children were concerned and Cecily's detailed descriptions of Thomas Richardson's behaviour had given her son an inherent fear of turning out the same way.

Sarah touched his hand. 'You're not your father. Any responsibility *you* take on you always see through. It's who you are.'

'How do you know?' Matt asked.

'Because my *Nonno* Enzo said you are a good man and he's right.' A brief laugh trickled out before she could help it. 'Unless you've got three ex-wives and a string of children you haven't told me about?'

Matt's wicked smile returned. 'Only two of each. Is that okay?'

The seriousness of the moment struck them at the same time. He slid his hands up to cup her face, dragging his thumbs tenderly over her skin and pulling her closer.

'Is that okay?' he whispered and Sarah managed to nod. This kiss was different. Yesterday was all heat, fire and desperation but now he took his time, trailing around the edge of her mouth and making her wait.

'If they claim they're only "good friends" now we're not going to believe them, are we Betty. I'm pretty sure they've put that ridiculous Facebook nonsense to rest.' Cecily's loud, strident drawl rang out and Sarah sprang back to her seat. Their mothers stood by the table wearing matching inane grins. 'Our very own Romeo and Juliet. Without the tragic ending of course.'

Despite everything Sarah laughed and was relieved when Matt joined in, throwing his arm around her shoulders and plainly giving up too. 'Balcony next stop?'

'Lead on Juliet.'

O Romeo, Romeo, wherefore art thou Romeo? This Juliet, on the balcony of the Casa de Guilietta in Verona, finds her own Romeo down in the street gazing up at her. But watch this space for a happy ending!

Chapter Eighteen

'You're brooding.' Sarah stood behind Matt and rested her head against his bare back. 'What's wrong?'

Talking was easier when he wasn't facing her. How could he possibly make her understand? Sarah's warm personality made everyone love her and what was there not to love? Matt jerked as her soft hair tickled his skin and she instantly took advantage and sneaked around to plant herself in front of him.

'We don't need to be clones for this to work.' Sarah snaked her hands in around his waist and pressed a lingering kiss on his mouth. 'If I'd wanted an affable, easygoing man who loved nothing better than chatting to people I wouldn't have fallen for you.' A hot blush lit up her cheeks. 'I didn't mean that the way it sounded. I mean …'

This time he did the silencing-by-kiss thing, only letting go when he was sure he could get a word in. 'You're right. But it's still difficult.' Matt pushed a rogue strand of hair away from her face. 'As a little boy I always planned what I was going to do the next day and I still prefer to have everything worked out in advance. Because of my father's behaviour and my own passion for work I came to the conclusion I'd never be any good at the marriage and kids bit so I ruled it out.'

'That's sad,' she whispered.

'Don't get me wrong. My mom's an incredible woman but I never saw a good marriage in action and my father was hardly a role model for the job.'

Sarah frowned. 'I know you'd prefer to have everything laid out in black and white. For us to draw up a contract with the terms spelled out. But life's messy. It doesn't often work that way.'

Matt didn't want to speak aloud the words that ricocheted around his head but one of them needed to and Sarah, with her relentlessly optimistic personality, wouldn't in a million years. 'You won't admit this so I'll have to.' Her lip wobbled and her vulnerability touched him. Matt ploughed on before he could lose his nerve. 'This isn't goin' to work long-term, sweetheart. You want, and deserve, things I can't give you.' Sarah's eyes flared with anger and her hand swept in a stinging arc against his cheek.

'You coward!' The accusation slashed through him. 'If you won't fight for something that could be bloody amazing you're darn right you don't deserve me. I've had one man who said he loved me and turned out to be a liar. I thought you were different,' she hissed. 'People assume because I teach small children and am usually good-tempered that I can't get good and mad. Well, I can. It doesn't happen often, but ...' Her voice trailed away and she stared at him in horror. 'Oh, my God.' Touching her fingers to his burning skin Matt saw huge tears well up in her eyes. 'Did I do that?'

'Yeah.' He tried not to smile. 'You're a little virago when riled, aren't you?'

'Don't sound so pleased.' Sarah's protest fell on deaf ears. It did his heart good to know he wasn't the only one with feet of clay. 'I don't understand what's come over me. I didn't get that mad when Tim left me for Althea.' The blood drained from her face leaving her skin almost translucent. 'What does that say about my marriage?' Matt guessed that she didn't expect a response. 'I'd known Tim most of my life. How can I possibly feel more for you after a few short days?'

Beats me. 'It's scary.' Feeble but true.

'You feel it too?' Sarah barely spoke above a whisper.

'Oh, yeah, I feel it alright.' Matt's raspy voice made her tremble. His piercing sapphire eyes never left her as his hands moved to her shoulders and slid off the blouse she'd put on to walk across the room.

When she'd woken up alone in his bed it'd hurt to see Matt standing by the window obviously brooding. She'd been on a cloud of happiness after Verona and they'd spent the long drive to Lucerne together on the bus. Betty hadn't even blinked when Sarah declared she was going to have tea with Matt in his hotel room and make their sightseeing plan for Paris. Her silence was a declaration of approval, not that Sarah needed it but it was good to have anyway.

'When's your next break from school?'

It was impossible to think straight while his hands trailed languidly over her skin, stroking and arousing everywhere they touched until she was on fire and begging him not to stop. 'July.' She gasped and his smile couldn't have been more wicked.

'Come to Nashville.' In one easy move he swept her up into his arms. 'I'll talk you into it. After.'

'After what?'

He gave a rough laugh, strode back across the room and deposited her on the rumpled bed. Slowly Matt lowered himself over her and Sarah reached up to wind her fingers around the back of his neck.

'After this, honey.' He ignored her plea for him to

hurry and took his lazy, sweet time. His rigid control heightened her pleasure and she could've wept with joy as he brought her along with him, knowing exactly when to hold back or pick up the pace. Matt captured her cries with his searing kiss and with a breathless moan filled her with everything he had. He wrapped his arms tightly around her and rocked them until the last ripples of pleasure died away.

Sarah took a mental snapshot of Matt, his beguiling eyes heavy with desire as he stared down at her, desperate to remember this moment when she was back home in Cornwall. Nashville was a dream. A wonderful one, but a dream all the same. She was supposed to be the dreamy, optimistic one but her practical, logical lover was the blind one tonight. For now she wouldn't force him to open his eyes.

Roger Clements had done it to him for the last couple of weeks and now Sarah was trying the same avoidance tactics. Roger's preferred method was to not respond to emails and phone calls whereas his lovely English rose was far more subtle. She favoured sweet seduction and Matt was only human. As soon as he mentioned the word Nashville again she kissed him all the way down from his mouth to the place where there were no brain cells to save him. After she'd worn him out in the best possible way she headed back to her own bedroom to save face with her mother.

His mother knocked and walked right in without waiting for an invitation. 'Are you ready for dinner?'

Matt stared blankly.

'You haven't forgotten it's group dinner night at a local fondue restaurant?'

Damn. The last thing he needed was to have to be polite to his nosy fellow travellers who would no doubt be watching his and Sarah's every move. According to his mother they were the most popular topic of conversation and Kayley, the chief matchmaker, was even taking bets on them.

Cecily sniffed the air and grinned. 'If I told them about this I could rake in some serious money.'

'About what?'

She wagged her finger in his face. 'Don't bother, Matt. I'd recognise Sarah's perfume anywhere. The bed is half-made. Plus you're looking distinctly bedraggled around the edges, although not as happy as I'd expect.'

Matt flushed with embarrassment.

'You want to talk about it?'

'Not really,' he mumbled. Since he'd become an adult they'd had an unspoken agreement to stay out of each other's private life. He didn't bring girlfriends home to meet Cecily and she kept her occasional hints about grandchildren to a minimum. In return he never asked his mother any questions when she went on a date or disappeared for the occasional weekend with a male friend.

'It's obvious she loves you.'

Is it?

'You'd be a fool to let her go.' His mother perched on the edge of the bed. 'Other people manage to work hard *and* have a life. It is possible.'

Matt shoved a hand up through his hair and stalked across the room to stare back out of the window. He couldn't bear to look at the crumpled bed pillows any longer. 'She doesn't think so and can't get her head around the long distance side of things. Sarah won't discuss it. She's very stubborn.'

'And you aren't?' Cecily laughed and he couldn't help cracking a wry smile. 'I'm going to give you some advice and then it's up to you.' Matt listened closely as she expounded on her theory. He was supposed to play it cool tonight, not exactly avoiding Sarah but making a point of appearing to enjoy himself and mixing with everyone else. Trying to play the part of a gregarious unconcerned man sounded appalling but his mother reckoned it would work so he'd give it a try. Starting tomorrow they had twenty-four hours in Paris before the tour finished and his mother swore if he couldn't win Sarah over in the most romantic city on the planet he didn't deserve her.

'That's it?'

She nodded. 'You'll have nearly sixty people on your side when we get there. I've heard several of their love stories and Sarah will too because I'll make sure they tell her. Every single one is different and that's what we need to get through to her.'

'We?'

Cecily's sly smile made him laugh. 'Haven't you heard it takes a village? She's been burned once, Matt.' Suddenly she turned serious. 'We've got to convince her to jump back in the fire.'

He found himself agreeing out of simple mathematical logic because he couldn't come up with a better solution.

Chapter Nineteen

Sarah dipped a square of crusty bread into the pot of hot melted cheese and popped it in her mouth. Sneaking a glimpse over at Matt she was puzzled. For a man who avoided crowds and conversation with strangers he was behaving very out of character. She'd saved him a seat next to her on the end of one of the long tables but he'd given her a cheery wave and chosen to join his mother in the middle of the loudest, noisiest group of their fellow travellers. Several times she'd heard his rumbling laugh and stared in disbelief. Was he trying to prove something, and if so what exactly was it?

'I've got a headache,' she lied to her mother. 'I'm going back to the hotel. An early night will do me good and it's not far to walk.' Sarah gathered up her linen jacket and handbag before sneaking out and leaving them all to their own devices.

'Don't you want a photo of us gazing at each other over the fondue pot?' Matt's hand stretched out in front of her barring her way out of the door. A drift of his musky aftershave teased her senses as he brushed against her shoulder. 'Or is game time over?'

Sarah shrugged.

'I'll keep it up as long as you want.' Matt's drawl thickened. 'I'll never break a promise to you, Sarah.'

'I know.'

He touched her jaw line, tilting it with one finger so she couldn't avoid his penetrating gaze. 'Do you?' When she didn't immediately answer a hint of sadness coloured his expression before disappearing again almost as fast. 'I'll see you in the morning.' Matt stepped away from her and before she could say anything he was gone and she was alone, again.

He hadn't been able to leave Sarah alone completely. It'd been the confusion shading her pretty eyes when she watched him laughing and swapping stories with the men of the BC group. Offering to take another photo had merely been an excuse before it morphed into something else. A question of trust. Maybe Enzo Agnoli was wrong and time *did* matter.

Not time. Timing you idiot.

Who could blame Sarah for not wanting to throw caution out of the window with him? He'd never even *thought* himself to be in love before. Never considered sharing his life with any woman. He tried to imagine how he'd feel if his imaginary wife left him for Clint and was now parading around Nashville heavily pregnant with his old friend's baby. *Shit.* No wonder she was skittish.

He couldn't go back in and pretend everything was fine because Matt wasn't up to trying to fool his mother or anyone else. Quietly closing the restaurant door behind him he debated whether to call for a taxi or walk.

'Matt, is that you?' Sarah's trembling voice came at him from somewhere in the darkness. 'Can you help me up?'

'Up where? I can't see you.' He hurried down the steps and pulled short a second before he would've planted his big feet right on top of Sarah lying in a crumpled heap on the pavement. The faint light drifting out from the restaurant showed her pale, strained face and the damp tears staining her cheeks. Matt squatted down by her. 'It's okay, sweetheart, your hero's here to rescue you.'

'I tripped and … oh, everything's wrong.' She sobbed and leaned against him. If it hadn't been for the fact she was obviously hurt he couldn't have been happier. To hell with his mother's stupid advice.

'I don't want to do any more damage. You sure it's a good idea for me to move you?'

'Yes, I do.' The sharp, schoolteacher tone of voice returned, convincing Matt she couldn't be too bad. 'For goodness sake don't let all of them fuss over me.' She grimaced and gestured towards the restaurant.

'Yes, ma'am. Your wish is my command.' Matt straightened his knees and leaned over to scoop her into his arms. 'I'm gonna call the hotel and get them to send us a taxi. I know I'm strong and you're a light weight but I can't carry you all the way back.'

'Put me down. I want to test my ankle.'

He cautiously set her on her feet but kept his arm around her waist. Sarah slumped and cursed under her breath as he steadied her by lifting the weight off the injured foot. 'No bad language please, young lady.' She stuck out her tongue and glared. 'Behave.' Matt sat down on the top step with her tucked into his lap and pulled out his phone. 'The manager's coming himself. It'll only be a few minutes.' He made a swift decision to tell her why he'd left the party. When he reached the part about finally understanding her better Matt sensed her smile against his chest. 'I'm not going to rush you …'

'But?'

If he was completely honest he might send her

dashing off again, metaphorically speaking since she couldn't actually run anywhere at the moment. But if he fudged things it'd put him on the same level as Tim the Louse.

'Mr Anderson? Ms Agnoli?' A dapper little man with slicked back hair and a thin moustache appeared out of nowhere. 'The hotel car is at your service. Do you need any help with the young lady, sir?'

'Nope, I'm good.' He stood up with her cradled safely in his arms, ignoring her hissed demand to let her walk. 'We're gonna get that ankle checked out first.'

'You're a bully.'

'Right back at you.' Matt silenced her with another kiss. 'I'll talk later. I haven't forgotten.'

Sarah's ankle throbbed but she refused to take the strong painkillers the doctor tried to force on her. After a thorough check he'd confirmed her suspicion that it was only a mild sprain.

'Rest, ice, compression and elevation, young lady.'

'Is there any problem with her travelling to Paris tomorrow?' Matt interrupted.

'Many long hours sitting in a bus won't be ideal.'

'How about if she can stretch out in the back seat?'

They seemed to have forgotten she was there but Sarah was too tired and sore to argue. She'd let Matt negotiate the terms of her release and argue with him later if necessary. Finally the men stopped talking and the doctor packed his bag.

'*Guet Nacht.*' Matt immediately responded to the doctor's farewell, spoken in the local Lucerne Swiss-German dialect. His language skills still took her by surprise although he was the sort of man who threw him himself into everything he did one hundred percent. She should've learnt that lesson by now.

Neither of them spoke for a minute.

'How long do you think we have?' Sarah asked and he checked his watch.

'They're having some sort of musical entertainment after the meal so we should be safe for at least another hour.' Matt's eyes shone. 'I assume you're not planning another roll in the hay in your condition?'

Sarah threw a pillow at him, hitting him straight in the stomach. 'Pig. You deserved that.'

'Yep, I guess I did.' Matt didn't sound in the least apologetic. His smile faded and he shoved his hands in his pockets.

'Sit,' she ordered. Immediately he selected a chair over by the door, far out of reach. 'Before you ask I don't need anything else.'

Matt raised one eyebrow, a trick she envied because it could convey a wide range of emotions with very little effort. 'In other words get on with it?'

Sarah shrugged. He'd told her not long after they met that he was too honest for his own good so now she was giving him the opportunity to prove himself.

'I promised not to rush you and I won't, but I need to tell you how I feel. Then it's up to you.' He cleared his throat. 'I'm hopeless at this.'

'Do your best.'

'I think I love you.' Matt's face flushed and he cleared his throat several times. If she wasn't so "nice" Sarah might be tempted to smile at his awkwardness. 'I've never said that to any woman before and I'm guessin' it's not the definite declaration you want but it's the best I can do right now, honey.'

'Will it help if I say the same in return?' she ventured. 'You have to get past the fact I *did* say it before. But everything feels different with you. More real. That's the best way I can explain it.'

He got up and came to sit by her on the bed, wrapping his arm around her shoulders and pulling her close. 'I think it's gonna take more than a day in Paris to seal the deal, don't you? I expect you hate me for saying that.'

Sarah shook her head. Of course she had romantic dreams of the City of Light, what normal woman didn't, but at nearly thirty and with a failed marriage behind her she knew that's all they were – dreams. 'I'm really tired. Will you stay until I fall asleep?'

'I'll do anything you want.' Matt murmured.

Sarah snuggled up against his broad chest and allowed her eyes to close. Surreptitiously she crossed her fingers under the covers.

Time is nothing where the heart is concerned. Matt was logical and sensible but she couldn't help hoping her grandfather would be proved right.

Chapter Twenty

Being treated like a piece of delicate china didn't suit Sarah. Between Matt, their mothers and a coach full of surrogate parents she'd been smothered all day. If anyone else offered her a pillow, an ice pack, snacks or a drink she was pretty sure she'd scream.

'I promise I'll whisk you away from them all as soon as we get to Paris,' Matt whispered, tucking a pillow back under her foot. The plan he had in mind would do that, and more, but it needed a few more finishing touches before tonight.

'You're just as bad!'

'Another hour or so and we should reach the outskirts of the city. Take a nap.'

Sarah sighed. 'If I do I'll never sleep tonight.' She'd taken several naps already out of sheer boredom and frustration. Straight through the drive from Lucerne would be about seven hours but with the usual multiple toilet and food breaks factored in today was dragging on forever.

'And the problem with that is?' Matt teased. 'I paid extra for a room with a view over the Seine.'

'All ready for seduction?'

'You know me better than that.' His words were laced through with hurt.

'I'm sorry.'

'Don't fret, honey, it'll work out.' He toyed with her hair, running his fingers through the loose strands and she ached to believe him. The rhythmic stroke of his fingers against the back of her neck stirred her senses and soothed at the same time and she gave in, lying back into his arms.

'Oh, sweetheart, look out the window. I promise it's worth waking up for.'

Still in a sleepy fog she struggled to focus. 'Oh, my goodness.'

'Pretty damn impressive, isn't it?'

'It certainly is,' she murmured, half to herself. Pressing her nose up against the glass Sarah greedily took in every aspect of the view spread out in front of her. Their promised drive around the centre of Paris raced by and the brief glimpses they got of the famed landmarks made her long for more.

'Everyone listening?' Kayley clapped her hands. 'Here's our hotel. You've got an hour to rest and freshen up. Be in the roof-top bar for our Speed Dating Finale cocktail party at five o'clock. The coach will leave around six to get us to the Moulin Rouge for dinner at seven o'clock. The show starts at nine and lasts for a couple of hours. We'll have a night tour of the city so you won't be tucked up in your beds until around one.'

'Would you mind skipping the Moulin Rouge tonight? I've got something more … intimate in mind. We've never been on a proper date.' Matt's soft drawl deepened and her breath caught in her throat. Was it shallow to find the combination of Paris and her new lover intoxicating? Sarah met his flashing eyes, dark as the midnight sky and equally mysterious, and couldn't refuse him anything.

'Yes.' She gave him a swift kiss and it didn't go unnoticed because a roar went up from the whole coach and everyone cheered. Pointed comments about

Paris being for lovers and what it must be like to be young ricocheted around until Sarah wanted to slide down to the floor out of sight.

'They're only jealous. I expect we'll be the same when we come back here in thirty or forty years.'

His calm assumption of their long-term togetherness stunned Sarah and she stared at him in complete bewilderment.

'Yeah, yeah, I know. I don't sound like the same man who spouted all that stuff earlier.' A quirky smile crept across his face. 'I guess it's a sign Paris can even work its magic on a hard-hearted, logical computer nerd.'

She hated when he put himself down and wished he could see all his good qualities for himself. 'Matt Anderson, you make me cross sometimes.'

'Only sometimes? Oh, heck, our jailor is on the way. We'll finish this later.'

Kayley appeared in front of them, hands on hips and wagging her finger. 'Get our lovely Brit safely off the coach and to her room.' She fake-glared at Matt. 'And yes I do mean *her* room. There's not enough time for any shenanigans before cocktail hour.'

'That's what you think,' Matt muttered under his breath and Sarah fought down the bubble of laughter threatening to erupt. Out loud he politely agreed with their annoying guide and helped Sarah to stand up. It took her a few seconds to stretch out her leg after lying down for so long. She brushed off his attempt to help and limped off the coach leaving Matt to follow along with their coats and carry-on bags.

'It's like trying to conduct a romance in a damn goldfish bowl,' he complained as they entered the hotel.

Sarah popped a kiss on his cheek. 'I must say you're the most handsome goldfish I've ever seen.'

'I'll feed you fish food tonight if you're not careful,' Matt retorted. Upstairs outside her room he pressed her up against the wall, leaning in for a long delicious kiss. 'Wear the slinky red dress again. I didn't get to appreciate it properly last time.'

'Whose fault was that?'

'You gonna give me a chance to make up for it tonight?'

Sarah tried to sound reluctant when she agreed but his instant smile – satisfied bordering on smug – told her she'd failed.

'Fair enough. Off you go.' Matt snatched her key card and used it to open the door.

Annoying man.

Matt stepped into the bar and allowed his mother to steer him towards a large group gathered around the trays of appetizers. She'd become friends with several other retired school teachers in their group and there was a friendly rivalry between them as to who knew the most about every place they visited. There was only an hour before he'd get a phone call from their chauffeur for the evening and he hoped Sarah wouldn't change her mind. Cecily thought her idea of getting their fellow travellers to tell Sarah their own love stories would soften her up and he hoped she was right. A sliver of hot red caught his eye and Matt gripped his hands to his sides as Sarah arrived with her mother. Betty avoided them and made sure Sarah ended up on the opposite side of the room. He struggled to be patient.

His mother nudged him. 'It's your turn now.'

He knocked back the rest of his martini. 'I'm goin' to rescue Sarah.'

'Good luck.' Not usually a sentimental women it surprised Matt to see tears in his mother's eyes.

'Thanks. For everything.' He gave her a quick kiss and turned away, coming face to face with the lady in question. Close up Sarah's beauty, an intriguing mixture of natural and flat out sexy, knocked him for six. Matt struggled to put together a sentence, hoping he wouldn't sound like a drooling thirteen-year-old boy trying to talk to his first crush.

'Save it.' Her crisp order made him smile. 'Get me out of here now.'

'Before you overdose on schmaltzy love stories?' Sarah's shock amused him and he hurried to explain his mother's devious plot. When she didn't laugh a pit opened in the base of his stomach. 'They meant well.'

'We're not children to be sweet-talked into romance. How on earth could you go along with it?'

'It's harmless. Are you still coming with me? I promise you'll love what I've got planned.'

'I'm only agreeing because I don't want to make a fuss.'

'Really?' Sarah's cheeks burned and Matt took a guess that her delicate skin was the same shade of hot pink all over. While she was still speechless he took a chance and tucked her hand through his arm. '*Bonne nuit, mes amis.*' He shouted goodnight, silencing everyone in the room and making Sarah stare at his un-Matt like behaviour. He started to hurry Sarah outside but just in time remembered her bad ankle and slowed down.

'Where are we going?'

'You'll find out.' His succinct reply obviously annoyed her because she kept asking over and over again while they walked to the lift, went down eighteen floors and entered the hotel lobby. 'Our car's outside.'

Matt swept her outside before she could ask any more questions. 'In you go.' A uniformed chauffeur opened the door of a sleek, black limousine and Sarah stepped into the back seat. Relief flooded through him. For a moment there he'd been certain she was going to ruin his carefully laid plans.

As they drove across Paris he kept the conversation light and relished Sarah's obvious enjoyment as she picked out the famous landmarks they passed.

'Everything's different when I'm with you,' he mused. 'Usually I'm completely focused on getting to a job on time and don't pay attention to anything else.' Matt drew her to him for a long satisfying kiss before letting go to peer out the window. 'I think we're nearly there.'

'Where?'

'Where we're going.' His enigmatic reply earned him a sharp poke in the ribs.

'Oh, heavens.' Sarah gasped. 'What a gorgeous place.'

'This is the Chateau Rochefort, the home of the ancient Eclimille family.' The driver said as they drove past an enormous rambling old house. He stopped the car on the edge of a lush expansive lawn. 'Your ride is waiting.'

'Ride?' She stared outside and caught her breath. 'A hot air balloon?' Sarah croaked.

'If you don't want—'

'No, no, you silly man.' She flung her arms around his neck. 'I've always wanted to go up in one. How on earth did you know?'

'Lucky guess, sweetheart.' Matt didn't want to admit he'd bugged her mother for ideas because he wasn't sure if that would count as romantic or too analytical.

Sarah got out of the car as soon as their driver opened the door and Matt quickly followed. She stopped still and gazed at the huge multi-coloured balloon, sighing with pleasure.

A smartly dressed older man came forward holding out two coats. 'I'm your butler for the evening and will be taking care of you. You'll need these. It'll be chilly once we get up.'

'Butler?' Sarah's cheeks burned. 'How wonderful!'

'Are you ready?' Matt asked and helped her on with her coat.

'Absolutely.' Sarah touched his cheek. 'I'll keep you safe,' she whispered. 'This is out of your comfort zone isn't it? You prefer to be in control.'

He nodded, equally pleased and disconcerted that she'd picked up on his nervousness. 'You've sussed me out.'

'If you'd like to climb into the basket we'll go ahead and get going. We don't want to miss the sunset.' Their pilot gestured towards the large basket.

Sarah took the lead and got in first. Matt sucked in a deep breath and clambered in with her.

'Goodness!' She stared at the small beautifully laid table and chairs ready for them. Matt hadn't realised until he checked online and found this particular business that you could even have dinner while on a balloon ride. It didn't sound very safe to him but if it kept Sarah smiling that way he'd swallow his concerns and say nothing.

'Champagne?' The butler proffered an open bottle and Matt grinned at Sarah's unquenchable enthusiasm.

Matt startled as the pilot fired up the burners and the loud roar made him automatically reach for her hand.

'It's going to be wonderful. The view will be incredible.'

He thought the view was perfect already from where he was sitting and didn't honestly think it would be improved by drifting around in an oversized basket with a fire over his head but managed to smile and agree.

'To us.' He raised his glass and mentally added his mother to the toast. If she hadn't insisted on taking this coach trip he'd never have met Sarah and his life would be a far greyer, duller place.

'Look, you can see the chateau. The gardens are stunning.' Sarah beamed. 'Oh look at the lake. It's like a mirror.'

He forced himself to take his eyes off her and look where she was pointing. With the panoramic view spread out beneath them he listened to her running commentary and forgot to be spooked.

Sarah savoured every moment. She'd expected dinner at a fancy restaurant, maybe even the Eiffel Tower, but not this. Matt was a terrible liar and the high colour in his cheeks when she'd asked how he guessed about her long fascination with hot-air balloons gave him away. There was no doubt in her mind that she had her mother to thank for this.

The thought of tomorrow sneaked into her brain briefly dulling her happiness. They would leave Paris and cross back over the Channel to England to end their tour. Sarah watched Matt unobserved for a few precious moments. The wind blew his unruly dark blond hair around and as he unexpectedly turned to face her the gleam in his scorching blue eyes tightened her heart painfully.

He planted a hard swift kiss on her mouth. 'This isn't the end.'

Sarah ached to believe him.

'I'm not dumb enough to make some grandiose gesture up here.' Matt shook his head. 'I know things will be different when we're back down to earth—' he grinned, '—literally and figuratively.'

'So what happens next?' Her voice trembled and she blinked back tears.

'We do the long distance romance bit until you finish school for the summer in July when I'll come to Cornwall.'

His pragmatism shouldn't have surprised her. That was Matt. A planner. Straightforward. No frills.

He wrapped his arms around her, close enough for her to feel his heart beating rapidly against her own. 'Then we'll be together.' The simple statement took her breath away. 'Don't ask for details. Not yet. I love you and you love me. It's enough for now.' An anxious furrow creased his forehead. 'At least I hope it is?'

Sarah smiled. 'Oh yes.'

'Right, I believe it's dinner time.' He gestured towards the butler hovering by them. 'Suddenly I've got an appetite.' Matt's mischievous wink made her blush and he bent over to whisper in her ear. 'We're going to make the most of every minute we have. Watching the sun rise over Paris from my balcony should be spectacular.'

Sarah didn't argue. Life was for seizing with both hands.

Chapter Twenty-One

Four months later in Cornwall

Long distance romance was tolerable and they'd survived the last few months with the help of modern technology but having Sarah back in his arms beat everything in Matt's book.

He'd been in Cornwall for a week now and fallen in love with everything about the beautiful area from the rugged coastline to the delicious Cornish pasties. Unable to wait another second he'd arrived the day after she finished school and they'd visited all the required tourist spots from Land's End to the Eden Project.

'Are you ready?' Sarah popped her head around the door.

'I sure am.' Matt said and reached out to pull her to him. 'Are you still okay with going?' They'd bumped into Althea yesterday while out for a walk and she'd timidly invited them to join her and Tim for a drink tonight in the local pub. To his surprise Sarah had accepted.

'No. But I need to do this.'

Matt brushed a soft kiss over her cheek. 'Let's go.'

In silence they made their way down the road and when they reached the Queen's Head Sarah threw him a brave smile before pushing open the door.

'I wasn't sure you'd come.' Althea hurried over to them along with a big, blond man Matt instantly recognised from the photos he'd seen.

'Nor was I.' Sarah's dry response broke the ice and they all managed to laugh.

'This is when I wish I wasn't pregnant,' Althea joked, 'a large glass of chardonnay would go down well now.'

'Tim Harvey I assume?' Matt stuck out his hand and they went through the usual polite introductions while sizing each other up.

The four of them settled around a table by the window with their drinks and made stilted, uneasy conversation until Sarah set down her empty glass. Two red circles bloomed on her cheeks.

'I'm really pleased to see you two looking so happy together.'

'Are you?' Tim asked. He fiddled with the beer mat and stared down at the table. 'I behaved badly, Sarah, and haven't ever apologised properly.'

'That's all behind us now.'

Matt admired her for taking the high road and had never loved her more.

'I'm glad you've, um, found—'

'Love.' Sarah said quietly but firmly, taking hold of Matt's hand. 'It was worth waiting for. I'm sure you'd agree.'

Tim flushed and muttered something unintelligible under his breath.

'Althea, you look tired.' Sarah said sympathetically and touched her old friend's arm. 'Why don't we call it a night?'

Matt took the hint that she'd had enough and quickly stood up. 'It was good to meet you both and good luck with the baby.' They said their goodbyes and he steered her back outside. 'All right?'

She nodded and turned to him with tears glazing her eyes. 'Thanks. You were wonderful.'

'I didn't—'

'I couldn't have got through that without you. Althea and I won't ever be close again but at least we can meet now without it being the end of the world. And I do really wish them well. For the baby's sake if nothing else.'

Matt smiled. 'I'm still glad you had the idea of pulling that Facebook stunt because I might never have snagged me the most beautiful, smart woman on the whole planet otherwise.'

'Flatterer.'

'Not at all.' He sucked in a deep breath, suddenly nervous. 'Can I ask you something?'

'Of course.'

'I don't want you to make any plans for the rest of the week because I've got a surprise in store for you.'

'What is it?'

Matt laughed. 'If I told you it wouldn't be a surprise would it?'

'I suppose not,' she conceded. 'I loved your last one so I'll trust you on this too.'

He knew she might absolutely love it ... or not. Matt would find out tomorrow.

'Why are we at the Newquay airport?' Sarah asked.

She'd enjoyed their hot-air balloon date but today's wild scheme was on a different level.

'To get on a plane.'

'Where are we going?'

'You'll find out when we're in the air.' His succinct

reply earned him a glare but he simply kissed her again and ignored it.

A private charter plane waited for them on the tarmac and Sarah's eyes lit up as they parked next to it.

'Doing things in style aren't we?'

'Why not?' She went quiet and Matt was afraid he'd overdone it. *Too late now.* 'You trust me?' Her gaze met his and she nodded. 'You won't regret it.' *I hope.*

Fifteen minutes later they were in the air and crossing Cornwall.

'Nashville!' Sarah shrieked. 'Are you out of your mind?'

It wasn't quite the reaction he'd hoped for but Matt reached for the open bottle of champagne and poured them each a glass. 'To us.' He held out one to her and she jerked it out of his hand, obviously still dazed by the stewardess's response to her question as to where they were going. 'Maybe I am deranged. But that's your fault.'

'My mother will call the police if I don't come back.'

Matt chuckled. 'Not gonna happen. She knows. So does my mom and they both think it's cool.'

Sarah drained her champagne in one gulp. 'You're all crazy. Totally mad.'

'We'll be having dinner soon and then we can sleep until we land in Nashville.' He gestured towards the back of the plane. 'There's a proper bedroom.' Matt lowered his voice. 'We can even join the mile-high club if you ...'

'I can't believe they let you kidnap me!'

He grinned and leaned back in the seat to reach behind him and pull out a small black suitcase. Matt laid it on the table between them, popped it open and watched Sarah's eyes widen. 'Your clothes. Make-up. Passport. All the essentials your mother thought necessary.'

'But …' She spluttered. 'We're supposed to be taking Mum back to Italy on Tuesday. We've got it all planned.'

'I'll have you back on Sunday. Three days. Not much to ask is it?' He reached out and grabbed hold of her hands. 'Please.'

'Why didn't you simply ask me in the first place?'

'Would you have come?'

'I'm not sure. You said you'd wait and give me time.'

Very calmly he explained this wasn't an attempt to force her into a quick decision. He wanted to show her his home and open her eyes to the possibilities before them. 'I didn't know any other way,' he murmured and caught the ghost of a smile in Sarah's soft brown eyes.

'Pour me some more of that delicious champagne,' she ordered. Matt mentally chewed off every fingernail while she took small sips and gazed around the luxurious plane. 'I must give you credit. You do know how to abduct a girl in style.'

He decided to take it as a compliment. Matt owed Clint big-time for coming up with the idea in the first place. *You gotta knock her socks off.*

Matt had been darn lucky she didn't knock his head off.

'Do you want me to ask them to turn the plane around?' He forced himself to ask, dreading she might say yes but needing to give her the choice. 'I will if that's what you want.'

Slowly she shook her head. 'I suppose now I'm here I might as well see it through.' It wasn't the most ringing endorsement for his plan but he'd take anything at this point. 'Don't I need a visa or something?'

'All sorted. Your mother and I went online and got the authorisation. It's all you require with your valid passport.' When he'd first had this mad idea it'd been the one thing Matt was afraid he wouldn't be able to pull off but thankfully it'd been more straightforward than he'd expected.

'I can't catch you out, can I?' Her lips curled into a smile. 'You said we were going out for dinner. I assume we're not talking about the usual plastic meals served on most flights these days?'

'Certainly not. Choose whatever you like.' Matt passed her the menu and allowed himself to relax for the first time since Clint suggested the whole bizarre scheme.

Sarah stirred and for a moment couldn't think where she was. A low rumbling noise hummed in the background while warm breath tickled the back of her neck. *Matt.* She half-turned and jerked up in the bed. 'Oh, my God, it's not a dream.'

'Hey, sugar, sleep well?' She couldn't resist when he kissed her, tickling her skin with his soft, fair stubble and making her giggle. 'We'll be landing soon so we'd better get dressed if we don't want to give the Customs and Immigration people something to talk about.'

People like her didn't fly across the Atlantic on private planes and drink champagne with handsome, wealthy American entrepreneurs. *And join the mile-high club in a king size bed on satin sheets.*

'You're the one doin' it again now,' he drawled. 'Thinkin' too much. I'm treating you to a short vacation. Nothing more.' Matt's stroking finger lingered on her mouth. 'I'm not sayin' I wouldn't like more ...'

'I get the hint.'

'There's a shower if you'd care to take one?'

She really wanted to resist all of this, but it was impossible. 'Fine.' Sarah refused to look at him again until she was dressed, catching his brief flash of disappointment because she abandoned the famous red dress she'd started off their evening in and changed into dark jeans and a jade green silky top. 'I thought it was more appropriate.'

'I suppose so,' he sighed. 'I'd better get ready myself. How about you ask the stewardess to rustle us up some coffee?'

'Trying to get rid of me?'

'Honey, if you stay within reach of this bed we'll both be in trouble.' His heavy-lidded gaze sweeping down over her sent a rush of heat zooming through Sarah's blood. The awareness that Matt couldn't keep his hands off her was intoxicating.

'Fair enough.'

'That's the Cumberland River. My condo is near the building with the pointy top.' Matt gestured out of the window as the plane flew in low over the city. 'Everyone calls it the Batman Building although it's really owned by a telephone company.'

His excitement was contagious and Sarah allowed herself to enjoy the moment instead of fretting about the insanity of what they were doing. She'd let Matt talk her into posting a Facebook picture of them on the plane drinking champagne. He'd listened to her protest that she'd put all that behind her and seen the stupidity of doing the revenge posts in the first place a long time ago.

'Do it for us. I want everyone to see we're happy. Nothing wrong with that is there?'

He'd been supremely satisfied when she couldn't come up with a decent argument.

'I've got it all planned what we're goin' to do. Tell me what you think.'

It was hard not to smile as he launched into a detailed itinerary for the next three days. He was treating her whirlwind visit to Nashville with the same thoroughness as opening a new branch of his business.

'I'm overdoing it, aren't I?' Matt slumped back in the seat.

'Yes, but that's okay. I'll tell you when it gets too much and we'll do the rest ...' Sarah's voice trailed away.

'Another time. I'll say it if you won't.'

'We'll be landing in ten minutes.' The stewardess interrupted them with a bright smile. 'The Customs and Immigration people will come out to the plane so you'll soon be off.' She left them and took her own seat in the back.

Sarah rested her head on Matt's shoulder. 'You're brave to take this kind of risk.'

'Hey, heroes are supposed to be,' he teased. 'Earlier I was pretty damn sure I'd rather face a fire-breathing dragon than you in full on angry mode.'

'Have you changed your mind?' Flirtation came easily around this man.

'Nope. I plan on keeping you happy so I'm not forced to do my St. George bit.' With that definitive statement and a swift, hard kiss Matt made his point.

'Welcome to Nashville.' The pilot's announcement over the intercom startled Sarah and her heart thumped wildly in her chest, the noise filling her head until she thought she'd pass out.

'Trust me.' His simple words unravelled the tight knot of nerves filling Sarah's stomach.

'I do,' she croaked.

'That's all that matters.'

Sarah nodded. She was tired of looking back. She was ready.

Chapter Twenty-Two

Everyone had been right. They'd tried to tell him something was missing from his life but until now he hadn't believed them. Matt watched Sarah sleep and forced himself not to touch her. He'd worn her out, hopefully in nothing but good ways, but the poor girl was exhausted and needed a break. Clint had grinned when he showed no interest in checking in at work although they had spent a few hours discussing Matt's idea of heading up their plans to expand into Europe.

He picked up a strand of her shiny brown hair and wound it around his finger.

'You couldn't resist, could you?' Sarah wriggled around to face him and Matt struggled to speak. Everything about her softened and glowed when she looked at him.

'Do you want me to?' Matt took the quick shake of her head as permission to kiss her again before settling her comfortably in his arms. 'Did you have a good nap?'

'Don't you ever get tired?'

He didn't think it was a complaint.

'What's next on the agenda?'

With her soft, warm body wrapped against him and rapidly stirring places that should've been worn out Matt didn't find it easy to give a decent answer.

'Apart from that.' A hot, embarrassed blush crept from her cheeks all over her body.

He'd taken her downtown yesterday and they'd walked for hours so she could get a sense of the city.

They'd spent some time in the Frist gallery and toured the stunning symphony hall before having a late lunch at the Farmer's Market. Last night she'd begged him to take her to the Grand Ole Opry she'd heard so much about, unable to believe he'd never been to a show there. But she'd made a point of saying it was the same in Cornwall where she took so much for granted and hadn't visited a lot of the popular tourist spots since she was a child until she'd shown him around last week. Sarah always left him feeling good.

'We can get out of town and see some of the countryside. Check out any of the old antebellum houses. Shop. Your choice.'

Sarah's eyebrows raised, she'd been practising doing just one but wasn't having any success except where it came to making him laugh. 'Goodness. All that power might go to my head.'

'Cheeky bugger. Isn't that what y'all say?'

'It doesn't sound right in your Southern accent.'

'*I* don't have an accent. *You* do,' Matt protested. They were having endless fun trying to straighten out some of the confusing language differences between them.

'To get back to the point. Today.' Sarah toyed with the hair on his chest and strayed lower. Matt counted from one to ten and back again in his head. The wicked shine in her eyes told him she knew exactly what she was doing. 'I think we'll have a lazy morning before you take me to some pretty little town for lunch and shopping.' She carried on stroking and Matt guessed she was on track to suggest something he wouldn't much want to do. 'I know we're both musically challenged but I'm a huge fan of the *Nashville* TV show and really want to do the country music thing tonight. I'd like to see some of the famous honky-tonks on Broadway, try line-dancing and maybe even karaoke if I get brave enough.'

'No problem. Whatever you want.'

Sarah's smile widened. 'You're a terrible liar, but I love you for trying so hard.'

Keep on loving me. It's all I want.

'I must buy some cowboy boots to take back with me when I leave.'

When I leave.

All the joy drained from the day.

Stupid. Stupid. Stupid. Why hadn't she thought before she opened her mouth? The idea of leaving Matt tore at her but they'd have to say goodbye again in two short days.

Silently she began to make love to him and his obvious anguish as they came together broke her heart. Every time he held himself still inside her and fixed her with his searing gaze Sarah died a little more. But they could never hold back on each other and the second he cried out her name Sarah was lost. Matt's damp cheek pressed against hers and they clung onto each other, silent again apart from their racing heartbeats.

A persistent buzzing noise came from the other room and Matt rolled off of her, cursing as he got out of bed and dragged on his jeans from the night before.

'I'll be back. Don't go anywhere.' The light, teasing comment was his effort to bring some normality back into the moment and she forced out a smile.

Sarah pulled the bedcovers back up and considered what to wear for their day out.

'Um. Change of plans.' Matt grimaced and quickly closed the door behind him. 'You might want to put on some clothes.'

'I was considering a shower.'

'Consider it after you've come out here.' He cleared his throat. 'We've got visitors.'

Sarah began to be annoyed. 'Don't shilly-shally. I suppose it's your mother.' Presumably Cecily couldn't wait to see if the plan to whisk Sarah off to Nashville had worked.

'Well, yes, but …'

She jumped out of bed and quickly tugged on the clothes she'd worn yesterday. 'Come on.' As she stepped out of the room it registered that he'd said "visitors" not "a visitor." *Too late now*.

'Mum!' She couldn't have been more stunned if the Queen was standing in front of her. 'What on earth are you doing here?' Instantly she regretted her rudeness as Betty's face sagged. 'I'm sorry. It's just a shock.' Sarah hurried over to give her mother a warm hug.

'I'm sorry too, love.' Her mother nodded towards Cecily. 'She thought it'd be a good idea but I wasn't so sure.'

'We couldn't be more pleased, could we?' Matt draped his arm around her shoulders and beamed. If Sarah didn't know him better she might even believe the outright lie. Cecily's smile tightened but she didn't give him away either. Betty was the only one fooled. 'We were planning to go off out to Franklin soon to do a little shopping and have a bite of lunch while we're there. You're welcome to join us.'

'Perfect,' Cecily declared, clearly not getting the hint. Only two more days and Sarah wasn't even going to get those alone with Matt. She could've cried. 'You'll love Franklin, Betty, it's a cute little old place.'

'Are you sure?' Betty frowned, fixing her attention on Sarah.

'Of course. We'd love you to come along.' What else could she say? 'Matt, why don't you make us all some coffee while I go and get ready? *Your mother's to blame after all. You sort it.*

'No problem.' He didn't blame her for being mad because right now he could cheerfully strangle his mother. Matt flashed Sarah a reassuring smile. He'd make this up to her if it killed him. 'Right. Coffee.'

He suggested his mother showed Betty around and whipped up some cinnamon toast while he waited for the coffee to brew.

'You're not happy with me, are you?' Cecily returned and he glanced over her shoulder. 'It's alright. Betty's sampling the delights of your fancy bathroom.'

This condo overlooking the revitalised waterfront had been an investment five years earlier and he'd got an interior decorator in to fix it up. The cavernous space with its excess of white walls, stainless steel and bare wood never felt like home until Sarah arrived.

'I thought it was a neat idea.' She shrugged.

Matt couldn't speak. If he did he'd say something he'd regret.

'Are things going well with Sarah?'

'They were.' His dry response hit home and a rush of heat flamed his mother's face. Matt didn't remembering ever seeing her blush before. There was no point beating this to death. 'It's done now. We'll make the best of it.' Matt switched into good host mode as Betty walked back into the kitchen. 'You have to try my cinnamon toast. It's one of the few things I can cook.'

'You mean you're not a gourmet chef?' Sarah rejoined them, fresh and smart in a cute blue and white dress. 'And there I was thinking I'd found the perfect man.'

Everyone laughed and made jokes about there being no such thing. Matt caught Sarah's eye and winked. They'd been surrounded by people for most of their short romance. He'd make this work if it was the last thing he did.

Chapter Twenty-Three

'You've always been a sensible girl. Is all this clouding your judgment?' Her mother waved her hand around Matt's luxurious home. 'Don't get me wrong,' she hurried on before Sarah could defend herself, 'he's a great man and you make a good couple, but ...'

'But what?'

'It's not our lifestyle, is it?'

The question hit Sarah hard and for a moment she didn't know how to reply. 'You know what. I'm nearly thirty. I'd love your approval but I don't need it.'

Her mother beamed. 'Good. That's the way it should be.'

'I don't get it.' Sarah couldn't hide her bewilderment. 'You said ...'

'My parents were wary of your father when I first brought him home. He was foreign and far too good-looking and charming for my mother's peace of mind.' A cloud of memory darkened her face. 'And don't say they were right. Maybe I wish he'd told me about his family but he couldn't have loved me more and I miss him every single day.'

Sarah touched her mother's hand. 'So do I.'

'Matt's a good man. I can see he loves you.'

She nodded. 'Grandfather Enzo said the same.'

'Everything alright?' Matt strolled into the room and glanced between them both.

'Absolutely.' Sarah jumped up and flung her arms around his neck. 'Couldn't be better.' She let go and went back to give her mother a hug. 'Thanks for everything.' Even the biting awareness of how few hours she had left in Nashville couldn't dim her spirits. 'I'm going to get changed. It's time to paint the town red.'

Matt's eyes sparkled. 'Is my favourite dress getting another airing?'

'Are you really so easy to please?'

'Yeah, do you have a problem with that?'

Not at all. Matt's straightforward honesty always left her in no doubt unlike Tim whose idea of being truthful consisted of telling her what he thought she wanted to hear.

'No, I like simple.'

'Good.' With her mother openly listening it was all he needed to say to make her happy.

Taking a breather Matt watched Sarah, Betty and his mother dance. Sarah would have blisters tomorrow. All the tourists who bought cowboy boots, put them on straight away and wore them for hours suffered the same fate, but she hadn't been able to resist pairing the flashy red boots embossed in gold with the famous dress.

After studying all the brochures and checking online she'd declared Tequila Cowboy to be their main destination for the night. They'd got the taxi to drop them off along Broadway so Sarah could shop first before hitting up a couple of bars. The club she'd selected should tick off everything on her list with its dance club, live band, game room and karaoke bar. Matt's only stipulation was that he'd do anything she wanted apart from ride the mechanical bull. No way was he risking utter humiliation *plus* life and limb.

'Oh, my gosh, that was so much fun.' Sarah flopped against him, breathing heavily. 'Can you get me another of those fun cocktails?'

'Is that a good idea?'

She screwed up her nose. 'I can't consider embarrassing myself at karaoke completely sober. You'd better get one too.' Sarah slid her hands around his waist and plastered herself against him. The heat and perfume rising from her body drove him crazy and he wished they were alone.

'You gonna let me go? I can't go to the bar with you attached to me like a limpet.'

Sarah pouted. 'Spoilsport.'

Matt made his escape and sneaked away to the "Wanna B's" karaoke bar to finalise his plans before going to the bar.

'Drinks, ladies.' He returned to find Betty and Cecily had managed to snag a couple of seats and were both fanning themselves in an effort to cool down. They'd tried to persuade him and Sarah to come out on their own but he'd insisted on them coming along. It'd puzzled Sarah but she hadn't questioned him. If he was going to humiliate himself in public he might as well do it in style. 'Next up karaoke?' His mother stared as if he'd lost his mind.

'You do know he can't sing a note?' Cecily warned, but Sarah only laughed.

'I can't either. It'll be fun.'

His mother picked up her glass. 'Come on. I have to see this. Pity I forgot my earplugs.'

'It would've been a good idea.' Betty joined in. 'The toddlers at her nursery school cry when she dares to sing.'

Matt seized Sarah's hand. He'd lose his nerve in a minute. 'Come on. This is on your wish list so we're doing it.'

Before he knew where he was they were hauled up onto the stage under searing hot, flashing lights with a rowdy audience cheering and stamping their feet.

'Don't we need to choose a song?' Sarah's tremulous voice told him she was having second thoughts.

'I already have.' Matt nodded over at the man working the controls and the sound of John Travolta and Olivia Newton-John singing "You're the One that I Want" blasted out. In his gravelly, out-of-tune voice he bravely started to sing, clutching Sarah and flinging his arms around as if they were on the amusement ride in *Grease*.

'You're mad,' she mouthed at him but finally joined in so he wasn't the only one being jeered and laughed at. Matt was relieved to realise she hadn't been lying about her voice. Once he caught his mother's eye and she winked. She knew exactly what he was up to.

As the song ended Matt instantly dropped to one knee and Sarah glanced wildly around before glaring back at him.

'What on earth are you doing?' she hissed, but he only fumbled in his pocket for the box he'd been guarding all night and opened it up. The square-cut diamond flashed under the lights and so did Sarah's eyes, brimming with tears. He hoped they were happy ones or he was going to look the biggest fool on earth. Matt's thumping heartbeat drowned out everything else and he focused solely on the woman staring at him with love written all over her face.

'Sarah Violetta Agnoli. You're the one that I want. Will you marry me?'

'Yes, yes, yes. Now for goodness sake get up before you make us look anymore idiotic.' She pulled him to his feet but Matt had gone past caring by now and grabbed her in a long, deep kiss.

He swept her up into his arms and carried her off the stage and out through the throng of people, to raucous cheers and clapping. Matt spotted their mothers and aimed for them. After he set Sarah back down on her feet she held up her hand to stop Betty and Cecily from hugging them both to death.

'Did you really just ask me to marry you?' Her serious expression bothered him.

'Yep.'

'Did I say yes, or am I imagining that part?'

'You did.' He lifted up her left hand. 'There's the proof.' For several, long agonising seconds Sarah didn't speak. 'My John Travolta dance moves did the trick. Next time you've got to wear a copy of Olivia's sexy black leather outfit.'

'Next time?' Her voice filled with horror. 'You. We. Are never singing together again in public or anywhere else. Is that clear?'

'Yes, ma'am.' Matt swept into a low bow. 'I couldn't top that performance.'

She shook her head, laughing helplessly. 'You certainly couldn't.'

'So we're all good?'

'I suppose so, but what about minor details like where we'll live, how we're going to …'

Matt kissed her questions away. It was rather like agreeing a business deal with a handshake and ironing out the contract details later. But he wasn't stupid enough to spell that out to Sarah. Instead he murmured about how much they loved each other and that everything else would sort itself out. He was getting better at making logic sound more romantic.

'I do have the honeymoon planned.' He slid his fingers down over the tempting red silk to rest his hands on the curve of her hips. 'It has to be another coach trip doesn't it? I'm sure we could get a discount if we agree to promote the European Speed Date tour in their next brochure. Plus we wouldn't know what to do on our own anyway.'

'Speak for yourself. *I* would.' Sarah fluttered her eyelashes and a sultry smile tugged at her lush mouth. 'You want me to teach you?'

'I'll be a very willing student. I always got straight As in school.'

'I bet you did, Mr Anderson.'

Matt chuckled and leaned in for another kiss. 'Champagne, I think, and another photo.'

In Verona I promised you a happy ending and here it is! My handsome beau surprised me tonight with this gorgeous ring and we couldn't be more in love. It's a good thing I've fallen in love with Nashville too as I'm sure I'll be spending a lot more time here in the future. Life is good.

Thank You

Thank you for reading You're the One that I Want and I hope you enjoyed travelling along with Sarah and Matt as they discover that seeing 7 countries in 10 days and lasting romance don't have to be mutually exclusive! Writing is a mostly solitary occupation and it's always a real pleasure to hear from my readers, my contact details are under my author profile so please get in touch. I know everyone has busy lives but if you have a minute to leave even a brief review on Amazon, Goodreads or the retail site where you purchased this book, it helps to spread the word about my books to other readers who might also love them.

There are a lot of great books out there and it's a privilege to know you spent some of your precious reading time on my story!

Love Angela

x

About the Author

Angela was born in St. Stephen, Cornwall, England.
After completing her A-Levels she worked as a
Naval Secretary. She met her husband, a US Naval
Flight Officer while being based at a small NATO
Headquarters on the Jutland Peninsula in Denmark.
They lived together in Denmark, Sicily, California,
southern Maryland and London before settling in
Franklin, Tennessee.

Angela took a creative writing course in 2000 and
loved it so much that she has barely put her pen down
since. She has had short stories and novels published in
the UK and US.

Follow Angela on:
www.twitter.com/AngelaBritnell
www.angelabritnellromance.com

More Choc Lit

from Angela Britnell

What Happens in Nashville

Book 1 in the Nashville Connections series

'What happens in Nashville, stays in Nashville!'

Claire Buchan is hardly over the moon about the prospect of her sister's hen party; travelling from the UK to Nashville, Tennessee, for a week of honky-tonks, karaoke and cowboys. Certainly not straight-laced Claire's idea of a good time, what with her lawyer job and sensible boyfriend, Philip.

But then she doesn't bank on meeting Rafe Castello. On the surface, Rafe fits the cowboy stereotype with his handsome looks and roguish charm but as he and Claire get to know each other, she realises there is far more to him than meets the eye.

Can Claire keep to the holiday mantra of 'what happens in Nashville, stays in Nashville' or will she find that some things are far too difficult to simply leave behind?

Visit www.choc-lit.com for more details, or simply scan barcode using your mobile phone QR reader.

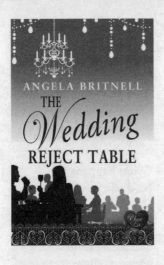

The Wedding Reject Table

Book 2 in the Nashville Connections series

Once on the reject table, always on the reject table?

When Maggie Taylor, a cake decorator, and Chad Robertson, a lawyer from Nashville Tennessee, meet at a wedding in Cornwall it's not under the best circumstances.

They have both been assigned to 'the reject table', alongside a toxic collection of grumpy great aunts, bitter divorcees and stuffy organists.

Maggie has grown used to being the reject, although when Chad helps her out of a wedding cake disaster she begins to wonder whether the future could hold more for her.

But will Chad be strong enough to deal with the other problems in Maggie's life? Because a ruined cake isn't the only issue she has – not by a long shot.

Visit www.choc-lit.com for more details, or simply scan barcode using your mobile phone QR reader.

Love Me for a Reason

Book 3 in the Nashville Connections series

Love doesn't always have to make sense …

When Daisy Penvean meets Nathaniel Dalton whilst visiting a friend in Nashville, it seems there are a million and one reasons for them not to be together. Nathaniel's job as a mergers and acquisitions manager means sharp suits and immaculate hair, whereas Daisy's work as a children's book illustrator lends itself to a more carefree, laid-back style. And, as Daisy lives in England, there's also the small matter of the Atlantic Ocean between them.

But when Nathaniel's job takes him to London to oversee the merger of a small publisher with a large American company, he and Daisy meet again under very different circumstances. Because Daisy works for the publisher involved in the deal, and if Nathaniel does his job, it could mean she loses hers …

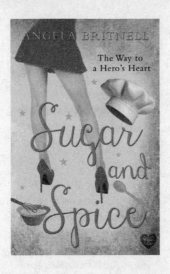

Sugar and Spice

The Way to a Hero's Heart ...

Fiery, workaholic Lily Redman is sure of two things: that she knows good food and that she always gets what she wants. And what she wants more than anything is to make a success of her new American TV show, Celebrity Chef Swap – without the help of her cheating ex-fiancé and producer, Patrick O'Brien. So when she arrives in Cornwall, she's determined to do just that.

Kenan Rowse is definitely not looking for love. Back from a military stint in Afghanistan and recovering from a messy divorce and an even messier past, the last thing he needs is another complication. So when he lands a temporary job as Luscious Lily's driver, he's none too pleased to find that they can't keep their hands off each other!

But trudging around Cornish farms, knee deep in mud, and meetings with egotistical chefs was never going to be the perfect recipe for love – was it? And Lily could never fall for a man so disinterested in food – could she?

Visit www.choc-lit.com for more details, or simply scan barcode using your mobile phone QR reader.

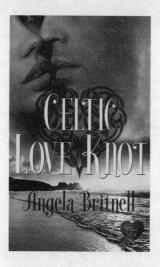

Celtic Love Knot

Can two tangled lives make a love knot?

Lanyon Tremayne is the outcast of his small Cornish village of St. Agnes. Susceptible to fits of temper and with a chequered past behind him, he could even be described as a bit of an ogre. But nobody knows the painful secret he hides.

Olivia Harding has learnt a thing or two about ogres. She's a professor from Tennessee, specialising in Celtic mythology and has come to St. Agnes to research the legend of a Cornish giant – and to lay to rest a couple of painful secrets of her own.

But when Olivia meets the ruggedly handsome Lanyon, her trip to Cornwall looks set to become even more interesting. Will she get through to the man beneath the bad-tempered façade, or is Lanyon fated to be the 'ogre' of St. Agnes forever?

Introducing *Choc Lit*

We're an independent publisher creating
a delicious selection of fiction.
Where heroes are like chocolate – irresistible!
Quality stories with a romance at the heart.

See our selection here:
www.choc-lit.com

We'd love to hear how you enjoyed *You're the One
that I Want* from our Choc Lit Taster range. Please
leave a review where you purchased the novel or
visit: **www.choc-lit.com** and give your feedback.

Choc Lit novels are selected by genuine readers like yourself.
We only publish stories our Choc Lit Tasting Panel want to see
in print. Our reviews and awards speak for themselves.

Could you be a Star Selector and join our Tasting Panel?
Would you like to play a role in choosing which novels we
decide to publish? Do you enjoy reading romance novels?
Then you could be perfect for our Choc Lit Tasting Panel.

Visit here for more details...
www.choc-lit.com/join-the-choc-lit-tasting-panel

Keep in touch:
Sign up for our monthly newsletter Choc Lit Spread for all
the latest news and offers: www.spread.choc-lit.com.
Follow us on Twitter: @ChocLituk and Facebook: Choc Lit.

Where heroes are like chocolate – irresistible!